"Be warned, I _____ ___ ____ for what I want," Mattie said.

"And what is it you want, Mattie?"

The way he asked the question, with that amber light glowing in his devil's eyes, made Mattie shiver. She was standing so close to him she could feel the rough denim of Hunter's jeans against her bare thigh.

"This is what I want," she said, lacing her hands behind his neck and molding her body to his. Their eyes locked, and she wasn't sure whether the thundering heart she felt was his or her own.

Lifting her head, she waited expectantly for his lips to crush down on hers. Instead, he lifted his eyebrow quizzically.

"Is this what you wanted, Mattie? Just this? I'm in need of something a little . . . stronger before rehearsal starts again."

She would have jerked away from him, but he suddenly locked his arms around her and hauled her roughly against him.

Then he kissed her right there on the brightly lit stage. But it wasn't really a kiss; it was an assault. It was Sherman sweeping through Atlanta. It was Joshua tumbling the walls of Jericho. It was Caesar conquering Gaul . . . and Mattie melted against Hunter, reveling in the heat of his embrace.

Bantam Books by Peggy Webb
Ask your bookseller for the titles you have missed.

WHAT ARE *LOVESWEPT* ROMANCES?

They are stories of true romance and touching emotion. We believe those two very important ingredients are constants in our highly sensual and very believable stories in the *LOVESWEPT* line. Our goal is to give you, the reader, stories of consistently high quality that may sometimes make you laugh, sometimes make you cry, but are always fresh and creative and contain many delightful surprises within their pages.

Most romance fans read an enormous number of books. Those they truly love, they keep. Others may be traded with friends and soon forgotten. We hope that each *LOVESWEPT* romance will be a treasure—a "keeper." We will always try to publish

LOVE STORIES YOU'LL NEVER FORGET
BY AUTHORS YOU'LL ALWAYS REMEMBER

The Editors

LOVESWEPT® • 203

Peggy Webb

Summer Jazz

BANTAM BOOKS
TORONTO • NEW YORK • LONDON • SYDNEY • AUCKLAND

SUMMER JAZZ

A Bantam Book / August 1987

If you would be interested in receiving protective vinyl
covers for your Loveswept books, please write to this address
for information:

Loveswept
Bantam Books
P.O. Box 985
Hicksville, NY 11802

ISBN 0-553-21830-1

Published simultaneously in the United States and Canada

PRINTED IN THE UNITED STATES OF AMERICA

O   0 9 8 7 6 5 4 3 2 1

To Terry, who walked all over Texas to find
    Winnie The Pooh;
to the staff members at the Lee County Library,
    who cheerfully research and answer all my
    crazy questions;
and to Sylvia, who has always wanted a book
    dedicated to her.

One

"Mattie's back in town."

Hunter Chadwick pretended he hadn't heard. He leaned closer to the tin soldier in his hand, turning it this way and that, inspecting the painted face, the miniature sword. But he wasn't really seeing the toy; he was looking backward in time, recapturing a summer ten years ago, a sultry summer of sea and sunshine and jazz. A summer of Mattie.

The voice of his toy designer continued on, providing singsong accompaniment to Hunter's thoughts. "Her granddaddy says she's a regular hellcat. Out all night, partying till Lord knows when, bringing in a parade of men that would make your head swim just to keep up with the count. She's got quite a reputation, that girl. Earned it in Paris, I guess. Remember that scandal about . . . ?"

Hunter nodded absently, but he wasn't remembering a scandal. He was remembering Mattie at eighteen, her hair wet from the sea and her long, tanned legs sugared with sand. He was remembering the way the sunshine brought out the amber in her green eyes. Cat's eyes, he used to call them. And how she had hated that! She would rail against him, calling him a spoiled rich boy, a lazy ne'er-do-well.

The old toy designer, with his wise little gnome's face and shaggy gray hair, gave Hunter a keen look. "I don't believe you've heard a word I said."

"Yes, I did. You said Mattie's back in town." Hunter placed the tin soldier on a marble-topped table, leaned back in his swivel chair, and propped his feet up on his desk. "And I don't give a damn."

That statement might have been convincing coming from anybody else, but in spite of his looks—his wild black eyes, bristling black hair, and intimidating size— Hunter was a teddy bear, lovable and softhearted.

And Mickey Langston, the venerable toy designer and Hunter's great-uncle, suspected Hunter cared. "Are you going to her welcome-home party? It'll be quite a berry mash, I'm told."

Hunter chuckled. Sometimes he thought Uncle Mickey's spoonerisms were all that kept him sane. "Merry bash or not, I'm not going. Besides, I'm not even invited."

"It's not until next week. And Phillip's feelings will be hurt if you don't come, it being right next door, and all. It's not every day a man's famous granddaughter comes home, you know."

Headlines flashed through Hunter's mind. "Mattie Houston, Jazz Sensation." "Jazz Pianist Takes Paris by Storm." "The Incomparable Mattie Wows London." He'd kept up with them all. Through the years he'd known exactly where Mattie was appearing, what songs she was playing, whose heart she was breaking.

His feet banged against the hardwood floor as he stood up. The vacated swivel chair spun crazily from his abrupt departure.

"Let's get on with this business of toy making," he said. "Mattie Houston is ancient history."

But she wasn't. The minute he heard the jazz later that night, Hunter knew he'd been lying. He was standing on his patio, surrounded by moonlight and cricket song and the sweet smell of gardenias. From across the hedge came the haunting melody, the shivers-up-the-spine blues, played as only Mattie could play it.

The music ripped at his gut, turned his heart inside out, and seared his nerve endings. The song was "Summer Wind." Their song. He stood rooted to the spot, scarcely daring to breathe, as the music poured over him. It was sunshine and laughter, wild summer rides and stolen summer kisses. It was sweet satin thighs and honeyed mouth. It was agony and ecstasy, promises and heartbreak, past and future. It was Mattie.

When the last strains died away, Hunter walked to the gap in his hedge and looked up. Mattie was there, sitting at the piano in the second-story music room, as he'd known she would be. Through the open French doors he could see her profile, classic and beautiful, unmarred by the years and the riotous living. Her dark blond hair, loose and flowing over her shoulders, was still long and streaked with gold and honey and flame.

She stood up and walked to the French doors, taking Hunter's breath away. The body that had driven him wild that hot summer so long ago was clothed in nothing more than a filmy negligee, so sheer, it might as well have been left in the closet. As Hunter gazed up at her, he felt like a starving man who had been invited to a sumptuous banquet. He couldn't get enough of her—the long length of leg, the tiny waist, the high breasts, upthrust and perfect.

Did she know he was out here? he wondered. Had she deliberately chosen that song? Was she teasing him?

He gazed at her without guilt. The lovely girl who had become a tantalizing beauty. The woman whose sweet kisses had lifted him to the mountaintop, then who had plunged him to the pits of hell. The delectable hoyden who had ripped out his heart and scattered little pieces of it all over Europe.

Sweat popped out on his brow, and he knew it wasn't from the heat. He lifted his hand in a mock salute. "To hell with you, Mattie Houston."

Then he turned on his heel and walked away.

When Mattie laughed she threw her head back, baring her delicate throat and setting her gold and flame hair aswing. She was laughing now, looking up at her adoring escort, tantalizing him with her dancing eyes and made-for-kissing lips. Suddenly the laughter stopped. Her face froze into a mockery of a smile and her hands became cold.

Hunter was here, standing in the doorway across the ballroom, bigger than she remembered, too handsome, too debonair, and much too real. She clenched her hands into fists and stiffened. How did he dare show his face? she raged inwardly. Who had invited him? Although ten years had passed, his shocking betrayal was still as vivid as if it had happened only yesterday. And it still hurt. Dammit all, it still hurt.

She hadn't realized she was staring, until Hunter looked her way. His mocking black eyes raked her from head to toe, setting her atingle with emotions she had thought long buried. She felt her nipples tighten against her gold lamé evening gown, felt the familiar surge of warmth between her thighs. Damn you, Hunter, she thought. Tossing her hair back defiantly, she returned his look. She assessed him boldly, as if she were planning to attack him and add him to the trophies hanging from her belt.

He acknowledged her gaze with a lazy smile. The smile evoked memories so powerful that Mattie wondered if some trick of fate had transported her back in time. The noise of the orchestra and the guests faded into the background. For her, nothing existed except Hunter and bright memories. She remembered the way the sun had looked on his bronzed skin, the sound of his laughter. She remembered the feel of his untamed hair, the taste of his wild kisses.

"Mattie, is anything wrong?" The voice of her companion penetrated her consciousness.

She tore her gaze away from the mesmerizing power

of Hunter and looked at her escort for the evening, Brad Something-or-Other. His name wasn't important. He was simply a means of forgetting.

She leaned over and kissed him full on the lips. "Brad, would you be a love and get me a glass of champagne?"

"Certainly, Mattie," he said, and hurried off as if he had been commissioned to save the world.

Mattie couldn't resist checking Hunter's reaction to her outrageous behavior. She tossed her head and sneaked a peek at him through the curtain of her hair. He seemed oblivious to her. He was bending toward his companion, an overdone redhead, smiling at her as if she were the only person in the room.

Mattie felt a tightening in her chest. The room was suddenly too hot. She couldn't breathe. Without a word to any of her guests, she left the room.

Heads turned as she walked toward the courtyard. There was no slipping out quietly for Mattie. Wherever she was, she created a sensation. The stunning beauty of her face and the glorious mass of hair were enough to give people pause, but it was more than that. Mattie had presence. Self-confidence oozed from every pore, and her unquenchable spirit seemed to reach out and grab onlookers.

Like the waters of the Red Sea, the guests parted, making a path for her to sweep grandly through. Whisperings and murmurings followed in her wake, but Mattie didn't notice. Getting air was foremost on her mind.

She swept through the French doors and across the courtyard. She didn't stop until she was almost to the gap in the hedge that separated her grandfather's yard from Hunter's. Her head felt light as she leaned against one of the stone columns outside the entrance to the formal flower garden. The stone felt cool against her flushed cheek. She closed her eyes and tried to regain her composure. She was Mattie Houston, she thought. She was rich and famous and talented. And scared.

She never should have come back. She should have sent someone to bring Papa Houston back to Paris for his birthday.

"Running scared, Mattie?"

Hunter! Although she hadn't heard his voice in ten years, she could have picked it out from a thousand others. Its deep timbre vibrated through her like a melody.

Lifting her chin in a regal gesture, she turned to face him. "I'm not scared of the devil," she said.

"Is that a fact?" The moonlight turned his eyes to glittering black coals, and he was impossibly handsome in his tuxedo. Age had improved him, she decided. The lankiness and uncertainty of youth had been replaced by solid muscle and a comfortable arrogance.

Casually he braced his arm on the column and leaned close to her. "Running away seems to be your style."

His well-defined lips were so near, the slightest movement on her part would put them in contact with hers. She drew a shaky breath and stood her ground. "That was a long time ago. Why the sudden interest?"

Hunter scanned her face, memorizing every small detail, cataloging it for later comparison to the Mattie he'd once known. The heady smell of gardenias almost suffocated him as she returned his scrutiny.

Suddenly he stepped back. "I'm just curious, Mattie. Whose heart are you planning to break this time?"

"Dammit, Hunter." She lifted her hand to strike, but he caught her wrist.

"You still have cat's eyes when you get mad."

"And you're still a spoiled child. Let go of my hand."

He released it and lifted his champagne glass in a salute. "To you, Mattie. I always did admire your spirit."

"It's a pity all that admiration had to be spread around."

"What in the hell does that mean?"

She leaned back against the column, needing its

solid support to remind herself that this scene was real, not a figment of her imagination.

"I have no intention of dredging up the past," she said. "I think what happened ten years ago should be left alone."

He raised his eyebrows. "Do you, Mattie?" He drained his glass, then tossed it over his shoulder. It shattered with a careless tinkle against the stone path. "Do you want to forget this?" He pulled her roughly against his chest, his eyes blazing down at hers. "And this?" He bent swiftly and took her lips in a punishing kiss. "And this?" His voice was harsh as his lips burned the skin revealed by the deeply slashed V of her dress.

By a supreme act of will she held herself erect, stiff and unyielding. But her heart betrayed her by its erratic pounding.

The kisses stopped as suddenly as they had started. Hunter drew back and stood as casually as if the madness had never happened.

"What are you trying to prove, Hunter? That you're irresistible to women? Your reputation seems proof enough."

"At least mine doesn't make headline news."

"That's one of the drawbacks of fame."

"When did the callous disregard for feelings come, Mattie? Before or after the fame?"

She slapped him. Her hand connected with a sharp sound that resounded in the quiet courtyard.

He laughed without mirth. "Is that any way to treat a guest?"

"I didn't invite you."

"Phillip did."

"I can't imagine why."

"He likes me. Always did. Even when I was a law-school dropout, planning to marry his teenaged granddaughter, Phillip liked me."

"That was his mistake. And mine."

Hunter's hand snaked out and lifted her chin. "But I came because of your invitation. 'Summer Wind.' "

Her eyes widened. "You heard?"

"And saw."

"I didn't mean for you to."

"Didn't you?" He let his hand drop to his side.

She opened her mouth to say no, but his eyes stopped her. They seemed to see through her brittle facade, to see past her glamour and her bravado. They seemed to burrow all the way down to the uncertainty.

She tossed her head, and her false laughter rang out on the summer night. "You caught me red-handed." She shrugged. "What can I say? All men are a challenge to me."

"Even me?"

"Especially you." Summoning all her courage, she touched him. For a brief moment her long, pianist's fingers played over his face, remembering the texture of his skin, retracing the squareness of his jaw, recalling the sensuous outline of his lips. "Yours is the heart I plan to break, Hunter."

She heard his sharp intake of breath, but he recovered quickly. "Then I'd be careful if I were you. This time yours might be the heart that's broken." He turned on his heel and walked toward the ballroom.

"Leaving without saying good-bye?" she called after him.

His steps slowed, and he turned beside the fountain. "I'm giving you a dose of your own medicine. How does it feel?"

"Better than betrayal."

He opened his mouth to reply, then changed his mind. She thought she saw a look of puzzlement cross his face, but it was gone as quickly as it had come. The splintered glass crunched beneath his feet as he stalked back toward the house.

Suddenly she felt cold. She shivered in spite of the hot summer night. Wrapping her arms around herself, she looked up at the sky. She had thought she was over him. She had thought time and distance had anesthetized her. But she was still vulnerable. When he had kissed her, a tide of desire had welled up inside her and threatened to spill over. How long had it been, she wondered, since she had felt that way, moist and ready and aching to be taken? How long since a man's touch had made her feel alive?

She shook her fist at the moon, a giant lemon cake in the sky, bright and frothy as only a Texas moon can be. "I'll show you, Hunter Chadwick. I'm not a scared eighteen-year-old kid anymore. I'll make you sorry you ever toyed with Mattie Houston's feelings!"

She ground the splintered glass under her gold slippers as she hurried back to the ballroom. She spotted Hunter immediately, dancing with that buxom, red-headed cow. With an amber light gleaming dangerously in her green eyes, Mattie crossed the floor and tapped Hunter's companion on the shoulder.

"You don't mind if I cut in, do you?" she asked. Her manner was so syrupy, it could have been wound around a fork. "Hunter is an old and very dear friend of mine." She signaled to a nearby waiter. "James, bring my guest a glass of champagne." The astonished redhead was speechless as Mattie moved smoothly into Hunter's arms. "Hello, darling," she drawled. "You forgot something."

"Did I?" His eyes danced with wicked glee as he pulled her so close, she could barely breathe.

"When I'm kissed, I prefer it French style." She lifted herself on tiptoe and wound her arms around his neck.

"Is this going to be a demonstration, Mattie?"

She didn't reply. Instead, she circled his lips with her tongue. "For starters." Her voice was low and sultry, like jazz. "Then this." She moved her mouth slowly back and forth across his, nibbling, tasting, teasing. "And this." With bold abandon she plunged her tongue between his teeth, thrusting into the warmth of his mouth until she roused his tongue to duel.

He held her in a crushing grip and came up for air. "Women who play with fire get burned."

"So they tell me." She took charge of his mouth

again, and it was exquisite torture. She felt the pain of resurrecting forgotten dreams and the pleasure of remembering carefree days. The kiss was a heady journey into the past, to a time of innocence and invulnerability, a time when the gold was still at the end of the rainbow. The kiss was an imitation of love.

When she could stand it no more, Mattie backed away. Hunter led her smoothly into a dance as if nothing had happened.

"Do you always require an audience for your performances?" he asked.

Mattie felt light-headed as she glanced around the room. Some of the guests, whose mothers had pounded it into their heads that it wasn't polite to stare, were dancing. Others were staring openly, not trying to conceal their curiosity about the famous jazz pianist who had scandalized Paris and seemed bent on doing the same to Dallas.

"Always," she said, tossing her glorious hair. "Next time I'll call the press." She backed off and patted him on the cheek. "You can go back to your painted doll now. Tell her that women with D cups shouldn't advertise the merchandise."

"At least she has a heart, Mattie." With that parting shot Hunter went in search of his date.

Mattie watched him until the crowd had swallowed him up. "I had one, too, Hunter," she said softly. "Once upon a time."

"There you are! I thought I'd lost you."

She turned and flashed a false bright smile at Brad What's-His-Name. He handed her a champagne glass, and she took a big swallow. "How can you lose me, Brad, darling?" she drawled. "I'm the star of the show. Mattie Houston, golden girl. Rich and famous and talented." And lonesome, she added to herself. So lonesome that sometimes she felt she was weeping inside.

She took another fortifying gulp of champagne, then kissed Brad. "Let's dance," she said. "Let's dance until our heads swim. Let's dance until the stars disappear and the sun starts to rise."

Turning, she aimed her glass at the ornate fireplace. It shattered against the cool pink marble.

"Let's dance until we forget."

But there was no forgetting. Hunter was always in her vision, leaning his dark head close to his companion, laughing at something she said, whispering in her ear, holding her head against his shoulder.

And Mattie felt betrayed all over again.

Two

"Aren't you coming in, Hunter?" Gwendolyn McIntosh turned the key and pushed open the door to her apartment.

Hunter looked at her without really seeing her. His mind was still on Mattie. Damn her for looking so gorgeous, he thought. Why hadn't she stayed in Paris?

"Hunter?"

His eyes focused on his date. Her red hair was limp from all the dancing, and her face had a petulant look. He wondered why he had ever thought she was fun. She was just another poor substitute for Mattie.

"Not tonight, Gwendolyn." He patted her on the backside and gently pushed her into her apartment. "See you later."

Gwendolyn knew better than to argue. Just being seen with Hunter Chadwick was enough to enhance her social status. Not every woman was lucky enough to spend an evening in the company of Dallas's most eligible bachelor. His reputation as a playboy was well known, however. She certainly had expected more than a pat on the butt.

She batted her eyes at him. "Not even one little ol' kiss?"

Damn that Mattie, Hunter thought. How could he expect to maintain his image if she kept interfering with his thoughts? Thrusting her firmly out of his mind, he smiled at his date. When Hunter smiled, the look in his black eyes was pure sex. Gwendolyn almost swooned.

"Certainly, my sweet," he said. "A kiss to dream on." He bent down and treated Gwendolyn McIntosh to a Hunter Chadwick special. It was a kiss so expert, so thorough, that only he knew it contained no feeling. It was a masterpiece of deceit. He had spread these kisses around Dallas by the hundreds. It was a kiss that had built his reputation. And when it was over, he always walked away unchanged.

"Good night, Gwendolyn." He got in his car and didn't look back. Sometimes he wondered if he wasn't becoming as mechanical as one of his windup toys. Except when it came to Mattie.

He struck the steering wheel of his Maserati. He had to put that woman out of his mind. As he whizzed toward home, he turned on the radio. Jazz filled the car. His fingers tapped out the rhythm on the steering wheel. Then suddenly he stiffened. Nobody played "Body and Soul" with that much command except Mattie Houston.

His face was tight as he switched off the radio and rammed a tape into the deck. He didn't even look at the label. Anything was better than another reminder of the woman who had walked out on him.

He hadn't meant to think about Mattie, but he couldn't seem to help himself. Maybe it was the music. Maybe it was seeing her again tonight. Whatever the reason, that summer of ten years ago crept into his mind. He had been twenty-six and Mattie only eighteen, but they had known what they wanted. She wanted a career in music, he wanted to become a toy manufacturer, and they both wanted each other. He gave her a ring and they set a wedding date. Then suddenly she was gone. No good-bye, no explanation. Nothing. Just the ring,

stuck in a plain brown envelope, delivered to his door
by Phillip Houston's butler.

Hunter's hands tightened on the wheel until his
knuckles turned white. "Dammit, Mattie. Why did you
come home?"

He floored the accelerator, racing home as if he could
outrun his demons. All the lights in his house were
ablaze. He smiled. Trust Uncle Mickey to spread out
the welcome mat.

Hunter gunned his car through the gates and roared
up his driveway. He slammed out of his car and strode
through his house, flipping off the lights. When he
reached his upstairs bedroom, he walked to the window. The Houston house was dark as a tomb. He
couldn't see a damned thing. Not that he was looking
for anything in particular, he assured himself. Certainly not Mattie. He just figured a light in the window
might mean Phillip was sick and needing help. After
all, he was getting old.

Hunter pounded a fist on the windowsill. Who was
he kidding? He was trying to see whether he could spot
Mattie and that brainless jock she had been swooning
over all evening. He jerked off his coat and tie and
flung them at a nearby chair.

It was as hot as a cotton field at high noon, and he
couldn't have settled down if he'd been under a court
order. He spun away from the window and strode out
of the room. Maybe a dose of night air would cure
whatever ailed him.

Without bothering to turn on the outside lights, he
walked onto his patio. It was shadowed with moonlight and fragrant with the scent of summer flowers.
He crossed to the gap in the hedge and looked at the
Houstons's darkened house. A belated attack of con-
science smote him. What had possessed him to act like
such an ass? he wondered. He'd earned that slap. And
more.

He grinned sheepishly. Even if seeing Mattie did tear
his heart out, he couldn't help but be pleased with her

spirit. Still the same old fire-breathing Mattie. Lord, how he'd missed that spirit.

A small sound behind him caught his attention. It was the unmistakable sound of water splashing. He turned around and peered through the dark toward the enclosed bower that housed his hot tub. What the devil was Uncle Mickey doing out here at this time of night? Suddenly he stiffened. A woman's sultry voice floated to him across the darkened patio, singing "The Man I Love." Mattie! No other woman could make music sound as if it belonged especially to her. The words were slightly breathless, and interspersed with tiny gulping noises. Hiccups or sobs.

With long, purposeful strides Hunter crossed the patio and entered his private spa. Mattie was sitting in one corner of his tub, alternately sipping champagne and singing. Her hair was piled on top of her head, water bubbled around her, and moonlight splashed her face and bare shoulders. She looked like a mermaid presiding over the sea.

"What the devil are you doing here, Mattie?"

With slow, languid movements Mattie set her glass down on the rim of the tub, tipped back her head, and looked up at Hunter. He was towering over her like a black fury.

"What does it look like I'm doing, Hunter?"

"Trespassing."

She smiled. "I'm relaxing. By invitation."

"Whose?"

"Uncle Mickey Mouse." She didn't notice she had used the affectionate nickname she'd coined for Hunter's uncle ten years before. "He said since Papa was too stubborn to install a hot tub, I could use his any time."

"He forgot to consult me."

She made a face at him. "Don't glower, Hunter. It makes you look like a grizzly bear instead of a teddy bear."

"I'm not glowering."

"Yes, you are." She waved a hand airily toward the

lounge chairs. "Sit down over there and try to smile, if you're going to stay. I don't want some old sourpuss ruining a perfectly good soak." She picked up her glass and took a large gulp of champagne.

Hunter ignored the chairs. "I don't intend to stay, Mattie."

"What's the matter? Afraid I'll seduce you?"

"On the contrary. I'm afraid I'll seduce you."

They were playing a game of one-upmanship, and they both knew it.

"Wasn't the painted-up redhead enough for one evening?" Mattie asked.

Hunter's smile was deceptively indolent. Seeing Mattie in his hot tub, her golden skin water-slick and shining, was almost more than he could bear. She evoked too many memories. His muscles tightened, and he crammed his fists into his pockets. "Her name is Gwendolyn, and she's no concern of yours."

"I'm not concerned. Just curious." She sipped some more champagne. "I'm surprised you even remember their names."

"I keep a little black book, Mattie. What do you keep?"

"Scalps. I have a few dozen hanging from my belt." She hiccuped into her champagne.

He bent down, took the glass from her, and set it on a nearby table. "You never could drink champagne."

She glared up at him. "Since when have you become my keeper?"

"Since you got into my hot tub."

"You're scowling again."

"You shouldn't be out here alone, anyway. Where's that boyfriend of yours? Gone to make a down payment on an IQ?"

Mattie affected another hiccup to hide her giggle. Hunter had expressed her sentiments exactly. But then, he always did have a knack for that, she thought. Why did he have to be so good-looking and so vital and so close? Damn that charm and those incredible black eyes. He wouldn't break her heart this time. No, sir.

She was wiser, more sophisticated. She'd play the game and walk away unscathed. No pain, no tears, no regrets. And no feelings. Most of all, no feelings. She'd learned that the hard way—from Hunter. Revenge would be so sweet.

She pulled her gaze away from his and reached for her champagne, forgetting that it wasn't there. "Damn you, Hunter."

He thought she was talking about the IQ remark. "Don't cuss, Mattie. You never used to cuss."

"One learns all sorts of things in Paris."

His jaw clenched and his fists threatened to tear holes in his pockets. He stalked to a lounge chair and sat down. "I can see this is going to be a long evening."

"You don't have to play watchdog. Go upstairs and dream about your precious redhead."

"I don't relish the idea of waking up in the morning and finding you floating face down in my hot tub."

"My, my. I didn't know you still cared."

"I don't. I just don't like messy situations."

She almost choked on her rage. "Pity you couldn't have had those scruples ten years ago." She was so shaken by the enormity of her feelings that she ducked under the water to blot out his face. How dare he say such a thing after what he had done? she fumed. She stayed under until she felt the pressure build inside her head. When she came up for air, Hunter was kneeling beside the tub, one knee of his tuxedo pants soaked and his face a mask of anger. Another emotion played on his face, too, something she would have called concern if she hadn't known better.

He gripped her shoulders so tightly, his fingers dug into her flesh. "Are you crazy? Get out of that tub before you drown yourself."

She pushed his hands aside and lolled indolently in the tub. "I have to intention of leaving. I haven't finished my soak."

"In that case, I'll have to join you." He stood up and quickly peeled off his shirt, tossing it carelessly onto the lounge chair. With his hand on his pants zipper, he hesitated, looking down at her.

"Don't worry. I've seen it all before," she drawled. But her bravado didn't stop the rush of heat to her face or the increased pounding of her heart.

Hunter assumed she was referring to the countless other men in her life, men whose names had been linked to hers in the papers. He stripped grimly, throwing his clothes in the direction of the chair, until he stood before her as superbly naked and unselfconscious as a Greek statue.

He remained standing for a small eternity, his body moon-splashed and his black eyes challenging. Mattie threw back her head and returned his look. The night was so still, they could almost hear the moon move across the sky. Nothing marred the deep purple silence except their harsh breathing and the far-off whirring of a cicada.

They were drowning in memories—memories of hot kisses in the backseat of his Thunderbird, of tangled sweaty bodies on a beach blanket, of hurried clutchings behind the hedges. All the awkwardness and purity and wonder of first love swept over them, and they were forlorn.

It was Hunter who broke the spell. He stepped into the hot tub, making small eddies as the water swirled about his body.

Mattie couldn't keep her eyes off him. At thirty-six he was powerfully built, at the peak of his form. His muscles rippled under his smooth, tanned skin. Hair as black as the untamed locks on his head made a provocative triangle from his chest to his groin.

She hiccuped softly. It was the only visible sign of her turmoil.

He grinned, and she could have shot him.

"What's wrong, Mattie? I thought you'd seen it all before."

"Shut up and sit down."

He did, but it didn't help all that much. At night the

lights near the bottom of the tub shone up through the water, illuminating everything in their path. Hunter was sitting directly above one of the lights.

"This soak was your idea, not mine," he said.

"I didn't intend to have company."

"Didn't you?"

"No."

"Then why did you choose my tub?"

"Mere convenience."

"Come now, Mattie. This is about as convenient as that song you played the other night." His black eyes searched her face. "For me."

"You egotistical, arrogant, two-timing playboy! Did it ever occur to you that professional pianists have to practice?"

"Wearing peignoirs and standing in front of French windows?"

"It's my house. I'll do as I damn well please."

"Your games won't work this time, Mattie. I'm immune to your charms."

"And I'm immune to yours." But not tonight, she admitted. Not with his much-too-desirable body spotlighted so well. And not with those black eyes, as bottomless as the pits of hell and as breathtaking as lovemaking, looking at her like that, as if he were ravenous and she a mouth-watering banquet. Now was the time for a dignified exit. Tomorrow would be soon enough for dangerous games.

She stood up, the water plastering her minuscule strapless bikini to her body.

"It's been a lovely evening," she said, "and I do hate to leave such good company, but I must go. I have an early date tomorrow with another of my admirers. Good night, Hunter."

She stepped from the tub and strolled off through the moonlight.

And not a minute too soon, Hunter thought. In a wet bikini at close range Mattie was as dangerous as a match in a parched forest. His arousal had been instant and dramatic. It mocked him through the lighted water.

"You shouldn't play with fire," he called after her, but he didn't know whether he was saying it to himself or to her.

Mattie didn't look back until she was safely across Hunter's patio and through the hedge. Then she turned and leaned her forehead against a night-dark oleander bush. Why had she done it? she wondered. Why had she gone recklessly to Hunter's hot tub? She had known that he would find her. Those black eyes of his never missed a thing. She pushed her wet hair away from her flushed face. If this was revenge, it wasn't so sweet after all. It hurt, almost as much as the betrayal.

She sighed, a forlorn sound in the lonely night, then turned away from the hedge and started toward her grandfather's house. Hunter was with her every step of the way, not the self-assured, ruinously gorgeous man in the hot tub, but a Hunter of ten years ago, a laughing, sweet teddy bear, an idealistic man with a pocketful of dreams, a charmer who had caught her up in his vision and promised her the world.

She put one hand up to shield her face as if she could shut out the visions. But still they came. The laughter, the kisses, the tender young love, and finally the ring. Then her mother had come back, charming, beautiful Victoria, the toast of three continents. Victoria, who had had it all—an adoring husband, a talented daughter, a successful career as a high-fashion model.

Mattie swayed, stopped, pressed her hands over her eyes. Stop it, her mind screamed. Don't replay the ugliness. Don't recall the damning words.

She forced herself to draw deep breaths. Slowly the visions began to fade. Don't look back, she told herself. Her mother was dead and Hunter was just an empty dream. All that was behind her now. Dallas was at fault. In Paris she could keep everything in perspective.

But here, there was a memory around every corner. She supposed she'd just have to march straight ahead and quit looking for the memories.

Squaring her shoulders and lifting her chin, she went into the house.

"Kee-yii!" Papa Houston leaped in front of her, arms raised, fists balled, legs in karate fighting stance.

"Papa, it's me!" Mattie pressed her hand over her fluttering heart.

"Hell's bells, girl. Don't you know better than to sneak up on an old man in the middle of the night? You're liable to give me a heart attack."

She laughed. "I'm the one who's going to have the heart attack. Why aren't you in bed?"

"Why aren't you?"

"I've been soaking in Hunter's hot tub."

"Damned newfangled contraption. Sitting on your tail in a tub of boiling water's not the way to release tension. Exercise!" He executed a perfect roundhouse kick. "That's the ticket."

Mattie reached out to catch him, then realized there was no cause for alarm. At seventy-five Phillip Houston was nearly as spry as he had been at thirty. He landed squarely on his feet.

"Papa, someday you're going to jump around the corner at the wrong person and get yourself killed. What if I had been a real burglar?"

"We wouldn't be having this conversation. You'd be flat on your back and trussed up like a turkey." He demonstrated a powerful side kick. "I've still got what it takes, girl."

Mattie laughed and took his arm. "You certainly have. Now, come to bed, Papa. It's late."

Phillip shook off her arm and studied her with his keen blue eyes. "I don't need babying, Mattie. Just because I didn't come to Paris this year for my birthday doesn't mean I've got one foot in the grave. Contrary to what your mother thought, getting old's no crime."

"Of course not, Papa. But it's after two o'clock."

He threw back his head and laughed, and Mattie was startled again at the strong resemblance between herself and her grandfather. They had the same high cheekbones, the aristocratic nose, the generous mouth. Age had streaked Phillip's red hair with silver and lined his face, but it had not dimmed his good looks.

"In my heyday," he said, "I was just getting started good at two o'clock." He winked at her. "I won't tell Mrs. Cleary if you won't. I don't know why I keep that old dragon around."

Mattie wasn't fooled by his pretended fear of his housekeeper. Mrs. Cleary was as starchy as leftover pasta and as formidable as an angry bulldog, but she watched after Phillip Houston with the same possessive love she bestowed on his house.

"You keep her around because she's the only one who can get you to stay in line. Heaven knows what you'd be up to if it weren't for Mrs. Cleary."

They walked through the back sun-room and up the staircase, arm in arm.

"Why don't you move to Dallas and keep me in line?" Phillip asked.

"Papa, we've been through this before. My career—"

"Your career will allow you to live anywhere in the world. Jet travel puts you within hours of wherever you need to be." He squeezed her waist. "With William and your mother both gone, there's no need for you to live off over yonder all by yourself."

Mattie couldn't help but smile. Phillip's favorite phrase for Paris was "off over yonder," and he rarely referred to his daughter-in-law by her name.

"I'm happy living in Paris."

"Are you, Mattie?" Phillip gave her a look that made her squirm.

Instead of answering his question, she leaned over and kissed his cheek. "Good night, Papa."

"Sweet dreams, my little Mattie."

His question haunted her as she walked into her bedroom. She had a wonderful career, a beautiful home, a loving grandfather, and plenty of companions. But was she happy? Was anybody happy? What in the world was happiness, anyhow?

She stripped off her wet suit and hung it in the bathroom. Without even bothering to shower, she crawled into bed and pulled the covers up to her chin. It was nearly three o'clock in the morning, and she was exhausted. Happiness would have to wait for another day.

Three

Mattie leaned toward her dinner companion, Clayburn Garvey, a well-known Texas philanthropist, and was rewarded with a gleam in his eye. She knew she looked good. The green silk dress bared her tanned shoulders and enhanced the green of her eyes. Her glorious hair, swept up into an artfully careless topknot, reflected the golden glow of candlelight.

But Clayburn wasn't the reason she was leaning forward; she was trying to get a better look at the man sitting at the table behind him. Hunter Chadwick caught her eye and winked. She lifted her wineglass to him in silent salute, then turned her attention back to her dinner date. She was elated. She'd chosen the restaurant deliberately, knowing Hunter would be there. Although it was his favorite restaurant, she'd left nothing to chance. Uncle Mickey had been her source of information.

Clayburn made a comment about the price of oil, and she laughed. Seeing the startled look on his face, she reached over and covered his hand with hers.

"I'm sorry, Clayburn. It wasn't what you said. I was thinking about something else—about Papa Houston and his karate," she lied. As she launched into the

SUMMER JAZZ • 25

story about Phillip's attacking her the night of her party, she kept glancing over Clayburn's shoulder at Hunter. He was the reason for her laughter. She'd plotted this revenge since their encounter in his hot tub. She could almost see the look of outrage on his face. She could almost taste the victory.

Clayburn wasn't fooled by her story. He had been her friend for too long.

"What are you up to, Mattie?" he asked.

"What makes you think I'm up to something?"

"This dinner. Of course I was flattered by your sudden invitation, but I'm too honest not to think there's more to it than my charm." He lifted his wineglass. "And you have that wicked look in your eye."

"You know me too well."

He laughed. "That comes from following you all over Europe. And you know it was more than music appreciation."

"Friendship."

"Yes. I finally settled for that. Would you care to tell me what's going on, and would it have anything to do with the man sitting behind me?"

"Yes on both counts."

"Watch him, Mattie. He has a reputation that's nearly as scandalous as your own."

She threw back her head and laughed. "Do you believe everything you read in the papers, Clayburn?"

"Which stories would you have me disbelieve, Mattie?"

"How about the one about me riding down the Champs Elysees in an open carriage, wearing nothing but a fur coat and pearls?"

Clayburn laughed. "I loved that one. Sounded just like you, Mattie. Was it true?"

"Do you think I'd tell and ruin an interesting reputation?"

"I especially enjoyed the story about you in Rome. All those priests, Mattie!"

"And an archbishop, too." She grinned at him over

the rim of her wineglass. "I'm just as wicked as I can be."

"You still haven't told me what this is all about." He gestured toward their fancy dinner table.

"Revenge."

He put down his fork and leaned across the table toward her. "Proceed."

"You need not know the particulars—just that I'm repaying an old debt. I feel as if my life has been on hold for ten years. If I can get this debt paid off, maybe I can get on with the business of living, really living."

"That sounds strange coming from you, Mattie. Most people envy you—your flamboyant lifestyle, your successful career, your pizazz. What more can you want out of life?"

"I don't really know. Maybe it's peace. Maybe it's joy. Maybe it doesn't even have a name. Perhaps it's just the satisfaction that comes from knowing everything in your life is in order."

"Could it be a reconciliation with the past?"

"How did you get to be so smart, my friend?"

"There have been rumors."

"One of the drawbacks of fame."

Clayburn held her hand. "What can I do to help you, Mattie?" He grinned. "Short of slaying dragons. I'm too old for that."

"Forty-five isn't old; it's prime."

"It's all a point of view, I guess."

She turned serious. "Set up a benefit concert for me, Clayburn."

"You must have read my mind, Mattie. Surely this isn't the help you want."

"There are strings attached. I also want to do a matinee for children."

"Done."

"There's more."

"Is that your way of saying, 'First the good part, then the bad part'?"

"I want the Chadwick Puppets to be in the matinee."

"No problem, Mattie. I think they're still available for occasional performances."

"I don't want just the puppets. I want the original puppet master, Hunter Chadwick."

"He hasn't done a show in the last nine years—not since the initial tour that launched his toy company."

"Get him. If anybody can do it, you can. But he mustn't know it was my idea."

"I can't make any promises, Mattie, but I will try. Are you sure you know what you're doing?"

"Does anybody ever know for sure what he's doing?"

"Probably not. Some of us just do a better job of pretending." He set his napkin beside his plate and signaled for the waiter to bring the check. "There's a good band at the club tonight. Care to go there and dance?"

"Thanks, Clayburn, but not tonight. There's something else I have to do here."

He settled the check and rose to leave. "I'll be in touch about the benefit. Take care, Mattie."

"You too."

She watched until Clayburn was out the door. Then she began the second part of her revenge. Arranging her face into the proper blend of friendly concern and sexual playfulness, she approached Hunter's table.

She noticed that he and his date for the evening, Miss Kathleen Forbes Clynton—don't forget the *y*—were almost finished with dessert. She'd come in the nick of time. Leaning far over Hunter's chair so that her cleavage showed, Mattie spoke close to his ear.

"Darling, how are you?"

He smiled with genuine pleasure. "Mattie! You look especially stunning tonight. Do you know Kathleen?"

"Who in Dallas doesn't? How are you Kathleen?"

Kathleen was always happy to be recognized, especially by a celebrity. She arched her neck, almost preening. "About to burn up in spite of this air conditioning," she said. All her *r*'s came out as *h*'s. "Dear Hunter has promised to let me cool off in his swimming pool after dinner." She fluttered her eyelashes at him. "Haven't you, sweet pookums?"

Mattie nearly giggled as Hunter cringed. She didn't know which he hated more, silly nicknames or exaggerated accents. She leaned closer and patted his cheek.

"And how's the injury, Hunter?"

"What are you talking about, Mattie?"

"Are you hurt, Hunter? You didn't tell me." Kathleen affected a pout.

Mattie pretended chagrin. "Oh, dear. Have I spoken out of school? Naturally, you wouldn't have mentioned it—I mean, it's so embarrassing and all—especially to Kathleen. Poor Miss Clynton. How could I have been such a dolt?"

Hunter was immediately on his guard. He knew damned well Mattie hadn't stopped by his table without a purpose. Furthermore, she was rarely embarrassed and never talked in run-on sentences.

"Mattie, what the hell's going on?"

Kathleen didn't take kindly to having her first question ignored. She asked the second in a piping, querulous voice. "What injury, Hunter?"

"I'm afraid I've already let the cat out of the bag," Mattie said. She bent over and patted Hunter's groin. "I broke it."

Hunter had a coughing fit. Mattie didn't know whether he was strangling back anger or laughter.

As for his date, Miss Kathleen Forbes Clynton, belle of Dallas society, puffed out her red cheeks, gasped for air a few times, then finally squeaked, "How?"

Mattie waved her hand. "I couldn't possibly embarrass you with the details. I'll leave that to Hunter."

She started to leave, but Hunter grabbed her arm.

"She broke it with her tennis racket," he said.

Mattie pulled against him, but it was useless. He had made a remarkable recovery, and had no intention of letting her have the last word.

"Oh, my!" the hapless Kathleen said.

"Hunter!" Mattie said.

He leaned back in his chair, keeping an iron grip on Mattie's arm. "Yep. We were playing tennis, and she hit the wrong ball."

"How—" Kathleen sputtered awhile, seeking a word descriptive enough for the awful thing she'd just heard. But she could find none. "Excuse me." She bolted from her chair and ran toward the ladies' room.

"Satisfied, Mattie?" Hunter asked.

She wouldn't have let him know her true feelings if he'd been torturing her on a rack. "I couldn't have done it better myself. I'm afraid I've put a terrible crimp in your plans."

He loosened his grip on her arm. "Nonsense. There are other ways."

"You're shameless."

"You knew that before you came up with this little scheme." He grinned at her. "I'm beginning to enjoy these exchanges with you. You keep me on my toes."

"I meant to put you off balance."

He continued as though she hadn't spoken. "Not that I'm condoning what you did to poor Miss Clynton. She'll probably never get over it."

"She'll survive. That woman has the fortitude of an ox and the vicious nature of a skunk."

"You hardly know the woman."

"Papa keeps me abreast of Dallas society."

"Tell me, if it's not too much trouble, Mattie, what was the purpose of that scenario?"

"To get rid of the competition."

"All you had to do is ask. I'd have dismissed them with a wave of my hand if I'd known you were interested."

Mattie knew he was teasing, but the look in his eyes was reminiscent of that long-ago summer. She decided to make a hasty exit. His look was far too dangerous.

"I prefer to do it my way," she said. "I like a good scandal."

"So do I. I guess that makes us a perfect match."

That look was there again. It almost took Mattie's breath away. She just wouldn't think about it, she decided. If she did, she might be tempted to abandon her plan, and she didn't want to do that. Once she made up her mind about something, she didn't like to back down. What was the worst thing that could happen? Hunter would make good his word and break her heart? That had already happened once, and she'd survived. No, she wasn't afraid of being hurt. She was more afraid of not being strong enough to exact her revenge.

"It doesn't make us a perfect match," she said. "It makes us perfect opponents." She left him sitting at the table and could feel his eyes on her back all the way across the room. That was exactly what she wanted. She knew Hunter. She knew his moods, his likes and dislikes. She knew what he admired and what he didn't. And most of all she knew how to make him want her.

That was all she intended to do, she told herself. Make him want her. No feelings involved. She'd eliminate all the competition and set herself squarely in his path. He'd want her. He'd want her so badly, he could taste it. Then—then she'd have her revenge.

She was smiling as she left the restaurant.

Hunter chuckled all the way home. Mattie was the mistress of outrageous behavior, he thought, and he loved it. Her antics had made the papers for years. She was famous as much for her behavior as for her talent. She was a unique combination of beauty, ability, and delightful wickedness, a once-in-a-lifetime woman.

The light was still on in the library. Hunter was in such an exhilarated mood, he didn't wait until he got to the room. "Uncle Mickey," he yelled from the hallway.

"In here," Mickey called.

Hunter burst through the library door, talking as he

went. "You won't believe what she did. By George, that woman has more brass than a brass monkey."

"Who?"

"Mattie."

"You always did admire a woman with spirit, Hunter."

"And gorgeous! You should have seen her tonight. She was breathtaking."

"She always was."

"She has more class in her little finger than all the Dallas society women put together."

"She always did. I never knew why you let her go."

A shadow passed over Hunter's face, then disappeared as quickly as it had come. Tonight wasn't the night for regrets. He'd had too much fun. He hadn't been this excited by a woman in years.

"Guess what she did?" he said.

"There's no need to guess. I can see you're tying to dell me."

And Hunter was. He didn't even notice the spooner-ism. With big gestures and frequent outbursts of laugh-ter, he told the story of what Mattie had done at the restaurant. "By now," he finished, "I'm sure Kathleen has told all of Dallas about my injury."

Uncle Mickey roared with laughter. "That must have been a blushing crow for your date."

"Only temporarily. Nothing's a crushing blow to Kath-leen. She was born with aplomb."

"Kind of like Mattie, eh?"

"Only in that respect. They're worlds apart in other ways."

"What ways?"

"Nobody has Mattie's zany sense of humor, her bold-ness, her vivacity."

"You admire the woman, don't you?"

"I did once." Hunter was thoughtful for a moment. "I guess I still do—in some crazy kind of way."

"Why'd you ever let her go?"

"I didn't let her go. She left me."

"What stopped you from going after her?"

"Pride. Youth. Who knows? It was a long time ago."

"Go after her now."

"It's too late."

"It's never too late."

"Yes, it is. There's no going back."

"It seems to me you have the rare chance to do just that, Hunter."

"Even if I wanted to—which I don't—I don't think it could ever be the same. I don't think a love that's been smashed can be put back together."

"Same people. Different love. Good night, Hunter. This old man's going to bed." Without further ado, Uncle Mickey left.

Hunter pondered his uncle's words. Same people. Different love. Was it possible? Could the two people who had found first love together learn to love again, but in a different way, a more mature way? He didn't know. He wasn't sure he would dare risk it.

He picked up a miniature carrousel music box, one of the best-selling items for Chadwick Toys, and wound it. The musical tinkle of "The Way We Were" accompanied his steps as he paced the room.

He'd taken many risks in his life. He'd shunned the path his father, Rafe Chadwick, a famous criminal attorney, had mapped out for him. Law was interesting—he'd even had a knack for it—but it wasn't what he wanted. He'd always wanted to be a maker of toys. Like his great-uncle Mickey, he had a fondness for the fanciful, the joyful things of life. He'd risked the censure of his father and an assured future by dropping out of law school and pursuing his dream. And it had paid off, handsomely.

He'd taken other risks, too, business risks. In a capricious market that seemed to rely on gimmicks, Hunter had maintained his leading position by keeping a large stock of ordinary toys that did nothing special except require a child to use lots of imagination. Also, he never hesitated to try the most fantastic, the most preposterous, new toy. That, too, had worked.

But risks of the heart were another thing. He'd loved and lost ten years ago, and for some reason, the hurt was still there. Underneath all his bravado and his reputation as a womanizer, he was a gentle teddy bear. He made a big show of growling and roaring, but he wasn't sure the teddy bear in him could risk being ripped to shreds by Mattie again.

He stopped pacing and picked up another of his toys, a jack-in-the-box. He pressed the spring, and out popped Humpty Dumpty.

" 'All the king's horses and all the king's men couldn't put Humpty Dumpty together again,' " he quoted. "Are you trying to tell me something, Humpty Dumpty?"

The little jack-in-the-box had no answer.

Chadwick Toys was housed in an old converted warehouse in downtown Dallas. For Hunter, going to work was like entering a wonderful land of make-believe. Toys of every size, shape, and kind rode the conveyor belts in the production lines. Some of the employees sang while they worked, others whistled, and still others kept the laughter going with their homespun stories. They reminded Hunter of Santa's elves.

He greeted them all as he made his way to Uncle Mickey's office. It was always his first stop of the day. He couldn't see his uncle amid all the clutter. Robots whirled around the room, cuckoo clocks ticked, music boxes tinkled, skater babies skated, dancing bears danced, airplanes flew, kites floated, and spaceships orbited. A giant castle in the corner presided over the wonderful craziness.

"Uncle Mickey, come out, wherever you are." It was a favorite greeting of theirs, stemming from Hunter's childhood, when he would put away one of the books his father had instructed him to read, and sneak upstairs to Mickey's room to see what wonders his uncle was creating with scraps of yarn and bits of fake fur.

"I'm in the boy tox," Uncle Mickey answered.

"What are you doing in the toy box?"

First the shaggy gray hair appeared, then the kindly old face, wrinkled like a sun-dried apple. "Looking for the oil. How can I boil that squeaking icycle if I don't have any oil?" He hopped spryly out of the box and bent over the bicycle that was leaning against his desk. "Did you come by to see my latest toy design?"

"Yes."

"It's up there somewhere." Uncle Mickey waved in the direction of his desk. It was nearly as cluttered as his workroom.

Hunter fished through the multitude of paper until he found a drawing, a precisely executed blueprint of a space traveler, complete with wings.

"I like it," he said.

"Of course you do. When you were a little boy, you used to talk about 'slying into fpace' someday. It's a universal dream. All the way back to Icarus, man has wanted to fly. Without a machine."

"If we push, maybe we can have this ready for the Christmas season."

Uncle Mickey looked up from the bicycle. "That's tight. You planning to work around the clock?"

Hunter just grinned. "We'll have a construction meeting this afternoon at three."

"We already have three new toys in production for the Christmas season. What's put such a burr under your tail?"

"With my reputation in shreds I won't have to bother socializing."

"Mattie's the reason, eh?"

"I wouldn't go that far." Hunter folded the blueprint, stuck it in his pocket, and gave his uncle a small salute as he left the office.

Uncle Mickey stared at the closed door for a full two minutes. "I'd go that far, Hunter," he said. "I would."

"Clayburn Garvey on line one," Hunter's secretary said.

Hunter did a few quick mental calculations. Garvey's name was well known. It was usually associated with oil, charity benefits, or horse racing. Sometimes all three.

He smiled. And more recently, he thought, with Mattie. He'd noted that Garvey was her dinner companion the night before. Nothing Mattie did escaped him.

He pressed line one. "Hunter Chadwick."

Garvey's noted, persuasive tones came over the phone intercom. "Hunter, I know you're a busy man, and I'll take as little time as possible. I'm planning a series of benefit concerts on the fifteenth of this month for the American Diabetes Foundation, and I want to include you and the Chadwick Puppets in the matinee."

"You have my permission, of course, to use the puppets. I'm always glad to help out. But you'll have to talk with Sarah, in our publicity department, about scheduling. I'll transfer you."

"Wait, Hunter. I particularly want *you*. This is going to be a big event—probably one of the biggest Dallas has ever seen. We're bringing in top talent. We want the best. And that includes the original puppet master."

Hunter smiled more broadly. He'd just bet they were bringing in top talent. Mattie, if he didn't miss his guess. He wondered if this was her idea and what the devil she was up to now.

"Who else will be in the show?" His voice was deceptively innocent.

"The matinee? Captain Kangaroo, Big Bird, Miss Piggy. It's going to be a hell of a show, Hunter. It'll be good for us, and it can't hurt Chadwick Toys if you agree to join."

"Mattie Houston."

"I beg your pardon?"

"You forgot to mention Mattie Houston."

"Well, I—" Garvey stopped. He was too shrewd to lie to Hunter. He reasoned that admitting Mattie was in the show wasn't the same as telling she'd requested Hunter. "How did you know?"

"Just an educated guess. She's in Dallas. I saw the two of you together last night."

"She's a sensational talent. Everybody is jumping at the chance to be in the same benefit show with her. I know you don't do puppet shows anymore, but if—"

"Yes."

"Is that a firm commitment?" Garvey knew when to shut up and close a deal.

"Yes."

"Great. I'll add your name to the list of celebrities. You'll get a follow-up letter about our first meeting to discuss rehearsals."

After Hunter had finished speaking to Clayburn Garvey, he stared thoughtfully into space. "Well, I'll be damned," he said aloud. He didn't know what had prompted him to agree to do the show. Was it curiosity or excitement or something else—the stirrings of some old, familiar feelings? Whatever his reasons, he'd given his word. And he never backed down on his word.

"Mattie, he's in." Clayburn Garvey said over the phone.

"How'd you get him, Clayburn?" Mattie tapped her long fingers on the musical score on her desk.

"It was the strangest thing. I really don't know."

"You must have given a real sales pitch."

"I did my usual spiel, but I don't think that had anything to do with it. Mattie?"

"Yes?"

"He knows you're in the show."

"How?"

"He's no dummy. He'd already figured it out."

"You didn't tell him I'd asked for him?"

"No."

"Good. I don't want him to get the wrong idea."

There was a silence from Garvey's end of the line before he spoke again. "Mattie, I'd be careful, if I were you. A man like Hunter Chadwick doesn't need someone else to give him ideas. You're playing with fire, and I don't want to see you burned."

Hunter had told her the same thing, she thought. Tingles of delight raised the hair on her arms and made her shiver. She laughed with exhilaration. "Don't worry about me. And don't worry about the show. My little plan won't interfere with the performance. You'll have to get a Wells Fargo van to haul off the money we raise."

"You're a trouper, Mattie. But just remember what I said."

"Thank's Clayburn. I will."

After Mattie hung up, she looked at the phone and smiled. The smile became a chuckle and the chuckle became an outburst of glee. She pranced around the room, chuckling and thinking all manner of outrageous thoughts. Her music was forgotten as she savored this moment of victory.

"I've got you now, Hunter Chadwick," she announced to the empty room. "Every day you'll have to see me at rehearsal. I'm planning to tie your heart in knots and feed it to the vultures. Yessir, that's exactly what I'll do."

She swept by the desk and picked up her music. She flipped the pages absently and continued her diabolical plans. "I'm going to make you fall down and worship at my feet. Then I'm going to tear out that two-timing heart of yours and scatter it all over Texas. Before I'm through with you, you'll wish you'd never heard the name Mattie Houston."

Still chuckling wickedly, she walked to the piano. She ran her hands lightly over the keys, rippling the treble notes, chording the bass. Her excitement flowed through her fingers and translated into a rousing jazz tune, a song of victory.

And while she played, she thought of Hunter. She imagined how he would look at her after she'd made him fall in love with her again—those eyes, black as Tar Baby, shining with that amber gleam of desire.

"Hunter." She didn't even know she had whispered his name. Without thinking, she segued into "Summer Wind." She leaned over the piano, caressing the keys, flowing with the melody, feeling the rhythm.

Awareness of the song gradually seeped into her consciousness, and she jerked her hands away from the keyboard. Why did that song haunt her?

She stood up and walked swiftly away from the piano. She wasn't afraid. She certainly wasn't afraid of Hunter, and she wasn't afraid of being burned. Nothing could stop her. If necessary, she'd wear asbestos.

Four

Every eye in the rehearsal hall was on her, and Mattie knew it. She was sensational, and she knew that too. Her music was electrifying. Her whole body was alive with it as she played.

Hunter was sitting in the front row, long legs stretched out, one arm flung carelessly across the empty seat beside him. He appeared to be paying no special notice to her, but she had glanced his way often enough to know that he was aware of every move she made.

She grinned. Things were going her way, she thought. She brought "Time on my Hands" to a rousing conclusion and winked broadly at Hunter. He acknowledged the wink by quirking one eyebrow upward. It wasn't much, but it was a start.

"That was great, Mattie. Stupendous!" The director of the benefit, Jo Ann Tyler, stood up and led the applause. She pushed her glasses up into her stylish mop of dark curls and consulted her note pad. "Do you want to go on, or do you want to take a break?"

"One more, Jo Ann."

The director turned to the other performers. "We'll take a break after Mattie finishes this one."

Mattie swiveled on the piano bench and looked down

at Hunter. "This one's for you." She spoke clearly enough for everybody in the front row to hear.

Jo Ann bent over her note pad, pretending she hadn't heard, but the two magicians craned their necks to get a better look at Hunter.

Once again Mattie saw his eyebrow shoot upward. Hunter was playing it cool, but she planned to shake him up a bit before the night was over. As she began the opening bars of "Temptation" she was very well aware that he knew the words. One thing that had attracted them to each other in the first place was his genuine love for music and his ability to sing along with most of the songs she played. He sang quite well, if she remembered correctly.

She grinned as he tensed and sat forward. He was getting the message, all right, she thought, gloating. The big question was, what would he do about it?

She wasn't long finding out. As soon as the song ended and everyone left the rehearsal hall, he jumped onto the stage and leaned against the piano.

"So I'm born to be kissed, am I, Mattie?"

She smiled. "That's what the song said."

"What do you intend to do about it?"

"I don't plan to stand in line behind every other woman in Dallas."

He chuckled. "If memory serves me, you have a rather unique way of annihilating your competition."

"I fight dirty for what I want."

"And what is it you want, Mattie?"

The way he asked the question, with that amber light in his eyes, almost made her lose track of her purpose. She did a light glissando on the keyboard for reassurance, then rose from the piano bench. She was wearing shorts, and standing so close to him that she could feel the rough denim of his jeans against her bare thigh.

"This is what I want." She closed the small space between them. Lacing her hands behind his neck, she molded her body to his. Their eyes locked, and she wasn't sure whether the thundering heart she felt was his or her own.

He used to love her boldness. She remembered how he would always pull her hips against his and capture her lips every time she touched him. Lifting her head, she waited expectantly for his mouth to crush down on hers.

Instead, he quirked that damnable eyebrow upward again. "Well, Mattie?"

"Well, what?"

"Is this all you wanted? If so, hurry up. I'm in need of some refreshment before rehearsal starts again."

"Damn you, Hunter." She would have jerked away from him, but he suddenly locked his arms around her and hauled her roughly against him.

"I didn't mention the kind of refreshment I had in mind." His smile was deceptively lazy. "I trust you were serious about being my slave, as the song says. I like my women willing and compliant."

And his lips took hers right there on the brightly lit stage. It wasn't a kiss; it was an assault. It was Sherman sweeping through Atlanta. It was Joshua tumbling the walls of Jericho. It was Caesar conquering Gaul. As his lips commanded hers, his hands pressed and molded her hips, moving slowly across the back of her denim shorts, wandering downward to caress the bare flesh below them.

Mattie was stunningly aware of his arousal. Her plan was working, she thought gleefully. She had Hunter in the palm of her hand. All she had to do was offer the body he knew so well, and she could do anything she wanted with him, including breaking his heart.

For a brief while her mouth moved expertly and mechanically as she kissed him, leading him on. But just when she would have backed away, triumphant and unscathed, her body began to betray her. She felt a sudden rush of heat, a frantic thrumming of her pulse. Her lips parted, and she found herself returning his kiss. To her mortification she became willing and compliant in his arms. She melted against him, reveling in the heated thrust of his tongue.

Revenge went begging. Betrayal was forgotten. The past didn't seem to matter. Nothing did except the one glorious moment when Mattie and Hunter kissed.

She knew it was insanity, but that didn't matter either. She felt as if she were standing in the center of a rainbow, its brilliance pouring through her veins, its radiance seeping into her soul.

Her hands crept up and wove into Hunter's untamed hair. The remembered feel of it, springy and alive and somehow very black, sent shock waves through her fingertips. She murmured his name against his lips and felt him smile. At first it was a small smile. Then it widened until it could no longer be contained.

Hunter was laughing. The kissing stopped as he threw back his head and laughed.

Mattie was furious. "Damn you, Hunter."

"That's twice you've said that, Mattie."

She would have pulled out of his embrace, but he held her tight.

"You're reprehensible," she said. She didn't know whether she was more furious with him or with herself. She was fast losing control.

"Why?" he asked. "Because I gave you what you wanted?" He tipped up her chin with one finger. "That was what you wanted, wasn't it?"

She bit back a hateful "no." Anger was no way to handle Hunter, she reminded herself. In order for her plan to work, she had to be what he wanted. He *did* like his women willing and compliant. But he also liked them with a touch of spice.

She forced herself to smile, hoping she'd combined just the right touch of playfulness and sensuality.

"It will do for starters."

"What else did you have in mind, Mattie? I'm willing to play this game."

"Right here on center stage?"

"Why not? We're both accustomed to publicity."

"I don't think Dallas is ready for what I have in mind." She moved her hips provocatively against his. Even through all that denim she could feel the heat of him. It almost made her forget her purpose—again.

Hunter caught his breath as he looked down at her. He held her tightly against him, savoring that well-remembered body for a small eternity. Then, abruptly, he let go.

"Dallas may not be ready," he drawled, "but I am. Anytime, Mattie. Just crook your finger. Or better yet, play that song again. 'Temptation,' wasn't it?" He reached over and traced her lips with his forefinger. "I'll add you to my list."

He walked away quickly, while he still could. He had thought he could play Mattie's little game and not feel a thing. He'd been wrong. He'd never wanted her more than at that moment. Desire raged through him with a force that nearly snapped his control. As he left her standing on the stage, he considered his narrow escape. He'd come too close to backing her through the curtains into a dressing room and taking her with all the fury of a summer storm.

"Just who was the tempted and who was the tempter in that game, Mattie Houston?" he muttered. But it didn't really matter. He felt an exhilaration he hadn't known since those sweet summer days when Mattie had been his love and Dallas had been his challenge.

He was smiling when he walked into the lobby. "I don't know what you're up to, Mattie, but you're on."

He didn't realize he'd spoken aloud, until Jo Ann handed him a glass of lemonade.

"Is it the custom of toy makers to talk to themselves?" she asked.

"Only the sexy ones." He looked at her over the rim of his glass. Damned if she wasn't a good-looking woman, he thought. She might be the perfect antidote to Mattie.

Jo Ann dimpled. "I've heard you were arrogant, but your conceit exceeds my expectations."

"I'm always happy to oblige a beautiful woman. Are you busy tonight?"

"I've also heard that you move fast." Jo Ann Tyler assessed him with her round, baby-blue eyes. "For you, I'll cut the rehearsal short."

"It's going to be a mite crowded in that bed," Mattie said. She moved in and linked her arm through Hunter's. "Is ménage à trois your style now, Hunter?"

He smiled down at her. "I'm game if you are."

"I'm more than enough for any man. Two would be superfluous." Mattie glanced significantly at Jo Ann.

Jo Ann's dimples faded. "When I'm directing a show, I like to keep it on a strictly professional basis. I hope everything has been satisfactory so far, Mattie."

"When everything's going my way, I'm easy to please, Jo Ann." Mattie's smile made the remark bantering instead of egotistical.

"Then there'll be no problem. Rehearsal will resume in ten minutes." Jo Ann Tyler took her dimples and her baby blues to the opposite side of the lobby and struck up an animated conversation with Captain Kangaroo.

"Care for a sip of my lemonade?" Hunter asked, offering his glass to Mattie.

"Yes. Being bitchy always makes me thirsty." She took a big swallow and handed the glass back to him.

He lifted it and ran his tongue over the rim exactly where her lips had touched. The unexpected sensuality of the move made her breath catch in her throat.

He lowered the glass. "Are you, Mattie?"

"Am I what?"

"Still more than enough for one man?"

Her heart caught when he said "still." Was he remembering or was it a slip of the tongue? Careful, she warned herself. This was a game, not a trip down memory lane.

She made her smile provocative. "Yes."

"What's to be the proving ground? My bed or yours?"

Her eyes widened. She didn't know why his boldness shocked her. He'd always been forthright and aggressive.

"What's the matter, Mattie? Scared?" His black eyes raked her boldly from head to toe.

"Certainly not." Her chin lifted as she rose to the challenge. After all, this was what she'd set out to do. If he moved things along faster than she'd imagined, that simply meant she could put all this behind her that much sooner.

"Good," he said. "From the look on your face, I was beginning to think I'd have to kidnap you."

"You'd do it, wouldn't you?"

"Yes. Since you've deprived me of one woman to-night, I see no reason why you shouldn't be a fairly good substitute."

"I'll make you eat those words, Hunter Chadwick."

"I'm counting on it, Mattie Houston."

"After rehearsal, then. Your bed." She walked away with more jauntiness than she felt. Playing this game was going to be harder than she had thought. Hunter was no ordinary man. His only consistency was in always doing and saying the unexpected. He was bigger than life, virile, vital. And he was almost sinfully handsome.

Mattie forced herself to walk into the rehearsal hall without looking back over her shoulder. Hunter was not an easy man to walk away from.

"Here's to you, Mattie," he said softly. "You're one helluva gutsy lady." His pulse drummed with excitement as he thought of the evening ahead. Whatever her game plan, he was fascinated. This evening was going to be very interesting, he decided. More than that, it might prove to be educational. He might even get a glimpse of Mattie's motives. Pillow talk sometimes loosened the tongue.

"I can hardly wait, Mattie." He was grinning broadly as he followed her into the rehearsal hall. But not for one second would he ever have admitted that his excitement was due to more than curiosity.

•   •   •

Mattie aimed her Porsche in the general direction of her garage and screeched to a halt. She hadn't stayed for the rest of rehearsal. Call it a brilliant move, she thought, a calculated ploy to make Hunter wonder what she was doing. Call it anything except what it was—cowardice. Seeing the Chadwick puppets again had brought back too many wonderful memories. How they had dreamed, she and Hunter and Fuzzy Wuzzy, his first puppet. How they had laughed, Hunter affecting a deep, rumbling chuckle for the puppet. No, she hadn't stayed. It had been too much.

She tiptoed into the house, hoping to keep from waking Papa Houston. But he bounded down the stairs, did a brief karate kata, and gave a karate bow.

She put her arms around his shoulders and squeezed. "Papa, you're incorrigible. What are you doing up? It's late."

"It's always late for me. I'm getting older every day, and I don't want to miss a thing." He kissed her cheek. "Especially not a minute of seeing my beautiful granddaughter. How was rehearsal?"

"Good."

"How could it be otherwise with my sweet granddaughter there?"

Mattie laughed. "Papa, I've never been sweet in my life, and you know it."

"Damn right. But when a fellow gets to my age, he can say anything he pleases—as long as he knows the difference between what's true and what's not." He chuckled as they walked together up the stairs.

"I won't be staying here tonight, Papa."

"You don't have to report to me, Mattie, but I hope to the Lord it's somebody I like. I didn't like that fellow you had at the party. Too much muscle. I never did trust anybody who looked like he could bench-press Texas."

"Neither did I."

"Then what in the heck did you invite him for?"

"Appearances. I have to keep my tarnished reputation intact."

Phillip stopped and put his hands on either side of her face. "Mattie. . . Mattie."

He spoke with such compassion that Mattie wanted to hide her face against his shoulder like a child. She wanted to pour out her frustration and her unresolved anger. She wanted to be weak. She wanted to transfer her burden to him. She was tired of being strong. She was tired of rationalizing for Victoria. She was tired of despising Hunter. She was tired of the gay deceit. She was tired of hurting.

Taking a deep breath, she shook off her weakness, blaming it on the tension at the rehearsal hall.

"Papa, don't you worry about me. I'm a tough little hellion. Cut from the same cloth you are. Besides, I'll just be next door. If I need any help, I'll simply yell for Uncle Mickey Mouse."

"You'll be with Hunter?"

"Yes."

Phillip was thoughtful for a moment. "I always did like that boy." He patted her cheek. "Good night, my sweet."

Mattie pondered over whether to change out of her shorts into something more seductive. She wanted to make Hunter desire her, but at the same time she didn't want to seem overly eager. In the end she decided on a fragrant bubble bath, the denim shorts, and a short-sleeved cotton blouse. Perhaps they would evoke memories of those wonderful, lazy days on the beaches ten years ago. In a burst of sudden inspiration she even scrubbed the makeup off her face and pulled her hair back in a ponytail.

She leaned close to the mirror and decided that in the dark she could still pass for eighteen. Almost. If you ignored her more-voluptuous curves and the tiny laugh lines next to her eyes.

She flipped off her lights and waited beside her bedroom window. She knew the exact moment Hunter's car turned into his driveway. Her hands clenched on the arms of her chair, and she sat forward to watch him enter his house. His walk was still cocky. She used to love that walk. She could pick him out in a crowd simply by his walk.

He tossed his keys into the air, caught them, and entered his house. She imagined that he was whistling. He always used to whistle. Sweat dampened her palms as she watched his progress through the house by the lights he turned on. Finally she saw the light in his bedroom window. He was there! Her heart pumped so hard, she could almost hear it.

Any minute now he would call. She looked at the silent phone. The minutes ticked by. Ring, dammit. Why didn't he call? Maybe he was waiting for her to call him. She reached toward the phone just as it rang.

"My bed's empty, Mattie."

His voice sent shivers down her spine. She licked her lips. "I'll be right over," she said.

"Hurry, Mattie. It's been a long time."

She gently cradled the receiver. Her hands shook. What did he mean—it's been a long time? Did he mean a long time since her, or simply a long time since he'd had a woman? Could it be that something had been missing from his life these past ten years? Could it be that his quest for love had been as futile as hers? Could it be that nothing and nobody had ever filled the emptiness after she'd gone?

Rubbish, she told herself. This was revenge, not déjà vu. Tossing her ponytail defiantly, she walked outside. "Look out, Hunter Chadwick. Here I come." And with those brave words she crossed through the gap in the hedge between her house and Hunter's.

Hunter stood watching at his bedroom window. Mattie looked glorious with the moonlight shining on her hair, he thought. Gorgeous. Seductive. Spirited. All the things a man could desire. Then why wasn't he feeling exuberant? he wondered. Something was wrong here. As he watched her walk across his patio he tried to decipher his feelings. Why wasn't he excited about having one of the most beautiful, most talented women in the world coming blithely to his bed? Because it was Mattie. That was the problem. With Mattie, sex had been more than a brief pleasure; it had been an act of love. It had been more than a mere coupling of bodies; it had been a joining of two hearts.

He struck the windowsill with his fist. Dammit. What was he going to do about this latent attack of scruples? He dared not show his vulnerability, especially to Mattie. She'd broken his heart once, and he'd be damned if she'd do it again.

In the halcyon days of their youth she had been so innocent, so trusting, so warm. Something precious seemed to shrivel up inside him as he heard her tread on the stairway. That was no innocent woman coming boldly to his bedroom door. His smile was cynical. So now the pot was calling the kettle black, was it?

He saw his door open. The die was cast. Now was not the time for silly sentimentality. The woman entering his bedroom was not the girl he'd loved ten years ago. She was as worldly-wise as he.

Mattie stepped into the room.

"What took you so long?" he asked.

"I can't sprint through that hedge as fast as I could ten years ago."

The way she said it, breathless and laughing, with an odd little catch in her voice, drove a shaft through Hunter's heart. Oh, Mattie, he groaned to himself. Don't resurrect the past. His gaze lingered on the freshly scrubbed face, the ponytail, and he was bereft.

He stood stiffly by the window, pulling himself together, telling himself that all the wishing in the world couldn't bring back their yesterdays.

"Has age also diminished your ability to strip?" he asked.

"No."

Her voice was throaty, sexy. She actually lowered her eyelashes when she said it. Her hands trembled slightly on the top button of her blouse. Watching her, Hunter decided she was a consummate actress.

He was wrong. Each button she popped open sounded like a thunderclap to Mattie. She was tense and uncertain, and she didn't know why. Now that she had Hunter exactly where she wanted him, she didn't quite know what to do with him. She knew how to make men want her, all right. She knew all the seductive moves, all the subtle glances, all the suggestive words. She knew how to retreat, too, how to leave them laughing and thinking they'd had it all. And how to keep them coming back for more. But this was Hunter, dammit. This was the sweet teddy-bear man who still lived somewhere in her memories in spite of the terrible thing that had happened.

She undid the last button and let her blouse slide to the floor. To her overly sensitive ears, its landing sounded like the clap of doom.

Slowly she lifted her face. Hunter was still standing beside the window, as remote and cold as one of Michelangelo's statues. And just as beautiful. For a moment the past and the present became one, and she felt such a surge of joy that she almost rushed across the room into his arms.

The ambivalence of her feelings shocked her. How could she feel joy in the presence of the man who had betrayed her?

Innocent, Hunter thought. Her eyes looked innocent. Why did she keep doing that to him? Why wasn't she acting bold and brazen and wanton? That innocent act was killing him. It was keeping him from lifting that flawless face to his and kissing her until her lips were bruised. It was keeping him from ripping that bra from her intoxicating breasts and drinking his fill of her. It was stopping him from throwing that miraculous body onto the bed and plunging into her like a rutting stag.

He hardened his heart.

"Take off the rest."

She licked her lips and slowly unfastened her shorts. They slid down her perfect legs and landed in a heap at her feet.

Mattie in black lace bikini panties and bra was enough to make angels turn in their haloes. Hunter had to sit down. He made a great show of pretended indifference as he sprawled in the armchair beside the window. He hoped the dark would disguise his almost-painful arousal.

"I'm waiting, Mattie."

She reached behind her back for the bra snaps. She felt cold. She felt lonesome. She felt small. And somehow she felt betrayed again.

Her hands hesitated. "You always used to help me with this."

Hunter couldn't stand it any longer. He didn't know whether she was acting, but it didn't matter anymore. What mattered was that he couldn't bring himself to take her as callously as if she'd never meant anything to him. He'd just have to do a little acting of his own. He flinched, stiffening his back.

"Damn!" he exploded.

"What is it, Hunter?"

"It's my back. An old injury." He wiggled his back and moaned.

"Lousy timing." She was smiling as she picked up her shorts.

"You can say that again." He stood up and made a great show of trying to loosen his back. "It happens sometimes. Damn the luck."

Mattie fastened her shorts and picked up her blouse, covering a giggle as she bent over. "Are you sure it's not that injury I gave you with the tennis racket?"

He grinned. "Would I con you?"

"I don't know. Would you?"

"I would no more con you than you would con me."

She laughed. "Then we're in trouble, Hunter."

"That was quite a show you put on."

"When?"

"Just now. That innocent act."

She started to say something, then changed her mind. Instead, she stood very still, watching him.

"It was a show, wasn't it, Mattie?" Deny it, he said silently. Tell me it was no show, Mattie. Tell me you still feel something for me. Tell me you can no more have casual sex with me than I can with you.

The appeal in his black eyes was so strong, Mattie almost told him the truth. She almost told him that what had started out as a game of revenge had become a dangerous attraction. She almost admitted that the old spark was still there, that something in her still reached out to him. But the truth would never do. She didn't think she could survive being hurt all over again. If Hunter had hurt her ten years ago, what would he do now, faithless womanizer that he was? No. The truth would never do.

She tossed her ponytail and put a gay lilt into her voice. "Of course, it was a show. I've learned all sorts of interesting tricks in the last ten years." Her reprieve made her brave. She walked toward him with a sway to her hips so provocative, it would have sobered Skid Row bums. Placing her hands on his shoulders, she leaned over and whispered, "When your back gets well, I'll show you a few."

At that moment Hunter could have choked her. He didn't want to hear about her tricks. He didn't want to know what she had become. Reading the headlines had been bad enough. He didn't think he could bear a demonstration. Something in him still wanted Mattie to be the innocent girl she'd been when he'd first known her. As unrealistic as it was, he wanted her to be the "good girl" he'd fallen in love with. Damned if it made any sense to him.

"Go home, Mattie." He pulled her hands off his shoulders.

"No."

"No?"

"That's what I said." She walked over to the bed and sat down. "If I go home, I'll ruin both our reputations."

"What do you intend to do?"

"Sleep here." She patted the mattress.

"Dammit, Mattie. You can't do that."

"Why not?"

He was temporarily at a loss for words. She grinned up at him. "Because it's my bed," he finally said.

"You can sleep here too. I won't bother you."

"Good Lord, woman." He paced the floor, speechless. Every now and then he smote the air with his fist.

"You've made a remarkable recovery," she said.

He stopped pacing. "What?"

"Your back. It seems to be all right now."

There was nothing else to do but laugh. He stood in the middle of the room and laughed at the ludicrous situation. Mattie's mouth tilted up at the corners, and then she was laughing too. Their mirth made it seem like old times.

"A pretty pickle we've gotten ourselves into," she said.

"You might say these two old con artists have outfoxed themselves," he agreed.

"What are we going to do about it?"

"One thing's for damn sure. I'm not sleeping in that bed with you."

"I didn't think you would."

"You're sure you aren't going home?"

"I can't. I told Papa I'd be gone all night. If I go home now, he's liable to think I'm an intruder and attack me."

"Phillip probably would." He chuckled. "Do you still like cartoons, Mattie?"

"I don't know, Hunter. I haven't seen Bugs Bunny in . . . a long time."

He opened a door in his entertainment center and rummaged around. "We've just shot a decent night's sleep; we might as well watch TV." He held two tapes aloft. "How does this sound to you—*The Revenge of the Road Runner?*"

Better than The Revenge of Mattie Houston, she thought. "Great," she said.

He put one tape into his VCR and walked toward the bed. "Scoot over."

"You aren't taking the chair?"

"No. I always watch TV from my bed." One side of the mattress sank under his weight. "Does it bother you?"

"No," she lied.

"Good. Who do you think's going to win?" he asked as the Road Runner and Wile E. Coyote began their battle of wills.

"Doesn't Road Runner always win?"

"Yes. But just once I'd like to see old Wile E. Coyote win. I'm going to bet on him." He turned up the volume. "Go get 'em, Wile E."

He was so like the fun-loving man she'd fallen in love with, Mattie thought. "I'll take that bet. You know you're going to lose, Hunter." She pointed to the TV. "Did you see that? Road Runner's already winning."

"That's okay. Don't you want to know what the wager is?"

"You made me forget to ask."

Hope rose in him. "How did I do that, Mattie?"

By being so like the gentle man I once knew, she started to say. *By being so close, you make me dizzy. By being so lovable, you almost make me forget the past.* But she said none of those things. "By acting so silly."

"Lady, you ain't seen nothin' yet." He hopped out of bed and pulled a tattered old mass of felt and fur from the top shelf of his closet.

"Fuzzy Wuzzy!" Mattie said.

"The same," Hunter said, affecting the puppet's deep, growly voice. "Who's that sleeping in my bed?"

She laughed. "I'm not sleeping, Fuzzy Wuzzy. I'm watching TV."

Hunter was delighted with her spontaneous response to the puppet. He continued the impromptu show. "Don't you know it's bad for your health to watch TV without eating? Have some potato chips." Working the puppet's hands, he whisked a bag of chips from a drawer of the bedside table.

"You still keep chips beside your bed?"

Hunter grinned. "Shh. Don't tell on us. Fuzzy Wuzzy and I like to eat in bed."

"Don't you dare drop a crumb," she scolded the puppet as Hunter plopped Fuzzy Wuzzy beside her and climbed back into the bed.

"I'm not worried about crumbs tonight," Hunter said, leaning against the headboard and propping his arms behind his head. "I'm not the one who'll be sleeping on them."

"You were invited." She reached for the bag of chips.

He caught her wrist and looked deep into her eyes. "Was I, Mattie?"

She didn't want to lose what was happening between them now, so she told him the truth. "Not really, Hunter. It was all a game."

"Why?"

"I can't tell you."

"Can't, or won't?"

"Both."

He turned her hand over and studied it. "Long, lovely fingers. Talented fingers." He bent his head and kissed the inside of her wrist.

The gesture was so tender, it made a small chink in the armor she had built around herself. "Don't."

"Why not?" He massaged her fingers.

"Because . . . you'll miss the cartoon." Deliberately she pulled her hand away. "See? Road Runner's winning."

She was freshly scrubbed and smiling. And he almost believed she was still his Mattie. "Why did you leave?"

"Did you see that rock fall on Wile E.? You're losing, Hunter." She pretended great interest in the cartoon, but he saw the fleeting look of pain on her face.

He called himself fifteen kinds of fool for waiting so long to ask the question he should have asked ten years ago. "I lost a long time ago. Why, Mattie?"

"Forget it. We can't go back."

The truth resounded in the still room like a dirge. They both heard the death knell of a love lost.

On the screen in front of them, Road Runner exacted his final revenge on Wile E. Coyote. Cymbals crashed and drums rolled as Wile E. met his fate beneath the screaming wheels of a train.

Neither spoke as the tape blurred into a gray nothingness. Finally Mattie, the consummate actress, tossed her head, setting her bright hair aswing, and smiled at Hunter.

"I won," she said.

He was falling in love all over again, he thought. Heaven help him, he was falling in love with Mattie.

His smile was bittersweet as he rose from the bed and punched the button to rewind the tape. "You certainly did win."

"Well?"

He turned around to face her. "Well, what?"

"Don't be dense, Hunter. What's my prize?"

He walked swiftly to the bed and bent over. "This," he murmured as he cupped her face. "A kiss for old time's sake."

His mouth was tender and undemanding and unbearably sweet. Mattie thought she had died and been reborn at eighteen. There was no probing tongue, no heated desire in the kiss, just gentleness and giving.

When the magic had ended, Hunter looked deep into her eyes. "We both won. Good night, Mattie."

"Good night, Hunter."

He left the room quickly, closing the door behind him. And Mattie shut her eyes and treasured the kiss in her heart.

Five

Hunter woke up at five. He felt as if he were balanced on the rim of a volcano, and at first didn't know why. Then he remembered. Mattie was in his house. Just down the hall. She was in his bed, hair tumbled, eyelashes lying on her peach-down cheeks, lips slightly parted in sleep. He saw her as clearly as if he'd been in the same room.

He pulled the pillow over his head and groaned. Why him? he wondered. Why hadn't she stayed in Paris and driven some other fool crazy? His heart thudded so hard, he could almost hear its beat.

He cataloged all the reasons he shouldn't fall in love with her again. She'd walked out on him once with no explanation. That made her unreliable. And faithless. She had a dazzling career, and he wanted a woman who was content to stay at home and raise his children. He wanted children, lots of them. And he might as well admit it. Thirty-six wasn't young. It was high time he got started on that large family he'd always wanted. But with Mattie? Lord, her reputation was as scandalous as his own. He wanted his children's mother to be as pure as the driven snow.

That last thought roused him to laughter. He sat up

and tossed the pillow across the room. He was about as pure as a tar bucket. He reckoned that if he wanted an old-fashioned good girl, he'd better get busy shining up his own tarnished image.

He crawled out of bed and pulled on jogging shorts. He'd grabbed some clothes before leaving his bedroom last night. No, Mattie was definitely not the woman for him. It didn't matter how he'd felt last night. That had been temporary insanity. In the broad light of day, he'd banish those foolish thoughts from his head.

He left the guest bedroom and walked down the hall. He was proud of himself for passing his bedroom without even glancing at the door. What did it matter that Mattie was behind that door, curled in his bed, gorgeous and desirable and cuddly-warm in her sleep? He stopped at the top of the stairs. Heaven help him, he couldn't go down.

Against his will, he turned around and walked back down the hall until he was standing in front of his bedroom door. His hand touched the knob and his senses reeled. He could almost smell the fragrance of her. He could almost feel her satiny skin, taste the heady wine of her kisses. He stood there, fighting temptation.

"Damn!" The muttered oath sounded loud in the quiet hallway. Clenching his teeth, he backed away from the door and hurried down the hall. Determination lent wings to his feet. He plunged down the stairs, through his front door, and into the early-morning stillness. Taking great gulps of fresh air into his lungs, he vowed to wipe Mattie from his mind.

He did his usual five-mile jog in record time and added a sixth mile for good measure, but still Mattie was with him. Back home, he stripped off his shorts and plunged into his swimming pool. His strong bronzed arms punished the water as he sought to banish Mattie from his mind and his heart. But still she was there.

Finally exhaustion forced him from the pool. He climbed out and stood on the tiled apron, his breath coming in ragged bursts. He knotted an oversized bath towel at his waist and raked his hand through his wild hair. His heart was pounding so hard, he wondered if he was having a heart attack. It had happened to younger men than he.

He sank into a lounge chair and tried to calm his breathing. He knew it wasn't a heart attack. It was Mattie. Why wouldn't she go away?

Burying his face in his hands, he groaned. The minutes ticked by while he wrestled with himself. Suddenly he laughed. He figured that he could either kill himself with exercise, trying to forget her, or he could go back upstairs and start all over again. The sanest move would be to go upstairs and start all over again. It might not be the *smartest* move, but at the moment it seemed to be the most necessary. Whether she was tarnished or not, he had to have Mattie. It was that simple. And this time he'd be damned if he'd let her get away.

"I hope you know what you're doing, Hunter Chadwick." He rose from his chair and went into the house. He bounded up the stairs two at a time, whistling all the way. He pushed open his bedroom door a crack and peered in just long enough to assure himself that the sexy bundle on the bed was Mattie, and not simply the tangled covers. Thank goodness she slept late. She always had. As he walked toward the guest bedroom he remembered how she used to groan and grumble in the wee hours of the morning when he would rouse her and sneak her back through the hedge. Those had been the golden days.

A small sigh of regret escaped his lips as he donned cut-off jeans and an old football jersey, faded evidence of his college-football career. No need to look back, he told himself. Mattie was not the girl she used to be, and he guessed that was his punishment for letting her get away in the first place. But not this time. This time he was going to keep her, even if he had to do it under lock and key. But first he had to win her.

Grinning hugely, he rushed downstairs to the kitchen and began the first phase of his plan.

Uncle Mickey was sitting in the sun-washed bay window, enjoying his coffee.

"Good morning, Hunter."

Hunter flung open the refrigerator door, rummaged around for a while, and emerged with four oranges.

"She likes her juice freshly squeezed," he said. He kicked the door shut and ransacked the cabinets for the juicer.

"I reckon I must be getting old," Uncle Mickey said. "Did you say something that I missed? Maybe I need a hearing aid."

Hunter grinned at his uncle. "Mattie. She's upstairs."

"Does that mean you're through with all this heating chart business?"

In his state of exhilaration, it took Hunter a second to realize that Uncle Mickey had meant to say "cheating heart."

"Yes," he finally said. Rich, golden juice squirted out of the oranges.

"Good."

"I won't be in my office this morning." He poured the juice and plopped two pieces of bread into the toaster.

"I thought not." Uncle Mickey added more sugar to his coffee and stirred. "Are you making a breakfast tray for Mattie?"

"Yes." Hunter buttered the toast, studied it critically, and added more butter.

"It seems to me Mattie has a soft spot for carrousels. If I were setting out to romance the woman, fly sox that I am, I'd put a music box on her breakfast tray."

Hunter grinned. "You're a genius."

"I know."

"Modest, too."

"Don't mean to be." Uncle Mickey stood up. "Seeing you like this almost makes me wish I were young again."

"Some wise toy designer once told me it's never too late."

"He wasn't talking about doddering old men like me."
Uncle Mickey squeezed his nephew's shoulder. "Good
luck, boy."

"Thanks." Hunter stripped off his football jersey and
turned his full attention to preparing the most delightful breakfast tray in all of Dallas.

Mattie's foot touched something warm and fuzzy. It
brought her awake with a jolt. She sat up, pushed her
heavy hair out of her face, and squinted. She didn't
adjust to morning quickly. First she squinted toward
the window to see if the sun was actually up. Next she
peered owlishly at the bedside table to see if the clock
was telling the truth. Then she stretched and yawned
to make sure her body still worked.

Everything checked out. That left the lump in the
bed. With her mind partially functioning now, she bur-
rowed under the covers to find out what was in bed
with her. It was Hunter's puppet.

"Fuzzy Wuzzy, you sly old reprobate, how dare you
sleep in a woman's bed uninvited?" She grinned at the
disreputable-looking puppet and smoothed his fur.
"You'll pardon my dishabille. It's the custom in Paris,
you know. It's supposed to drive men crazy. Of course,
I expected to be practicing my wiles on the puppet
master, not the puppet."

She became thoughtful. Propping herself against the
pillows, she pulled the sheet over her naked breasts
and surveyed the room. Hunter's room. She remembered it so well. It had changed a little. The chair by
the window was new. The curtains and bedspread were
different. How she used to love waking up in the morning with Hunter tickling her nose and urging her to
hurry before the sun came up. One morning as they
sneaked her back through the hedge, Uncle Mickey
had seen them from the pool. But he'd pretended not
to notice. After that, Hunter had started coming to
Papa's, climbing the magnolia tree outside her window

and climbing in like a fairy-tale prince. How they'd laughed.

Mattie sighed. No use reminiscing over the good old days, she reasoned. She'd been sidetracked last night by Hunter's cartoons and his antics with the puppet, but she wouldn't let that happen again. She'd almost believed he was still the tender, whimsical man she'd once loved. She'd almost been persuaded that love had not died, that it had merely been in hiding for ten years.

"I must have been out of my mind," she told Fuzzy Wuzzy. "He's tender, all right. With every woman in Dallas. No wonder I practically fell under his spell. He's certainly had plenty of practice with his technique." She propped the puppet on her knees. "That won't happen again. Mattie Houston is after satisfaction, not another broken heart."

"Fuzzy Wuzzy has never looked so good."

She spun around so fast, the puppet fell off her knees. Hunter was standing in the doorway, balancing a silver tray in one hand and holding the handle of a red wagon with the other.

"Don't you believe in knocking?" She tried to make her voice stern. She tried to remember her need for revenge. She tried to harden her heart. But Hunter looked so delicious standing there in his cut-off jeans, with that bronzed chest glistening in the early-morning sun, she could do no more than smile.

"Room service, Mattie."

She started to bolt out of bed, then recalled that she was wearing nothing under the sheet. She caught it just as it slipped over one breast.

"Don't you dare come into my room." She pulled the sheet up under her neck and tried to look prim.

Hunter was immensely pleased with the view. With her green eyes shining from sleep and her glorious hair tumbled about her, Mattie looked like a woman who had been thoroughly loved. "My room," he said. "Do get up, lazy bones. I like my coffee with you naked."

"I prefer breakfast in bed."

"As a matter of fact, I prefer you in bed myself. I may keep you there." He entered the room, pulling the red wagon behind him. It was loaded with gardenias and carrousel music boxes.

To Mattie's astonishment, Hunter set the breakfast tray on the bedside table and began to wind up all the music boxes. Miniature horses spun around to a tinkling cacophony of melodies. "The Way We Were" competed with "Deep Purple." "We're Off To See The Wizard" tried to drown out "Dixie." Melodies from *Oklahoma, South Pacific,* and *My Fair Lady* joined the discordant music.

Mattie was transported back to a time of dreams and enchantment. As she watched, Hunter set the last music box in place and strewed the gardenias across the bed. Their fragrance permeated her senses and seemed to clutch at her heart.

"What are you doing?" she whispered.

"Don't you know?" He sat on the edge of the bed. Looking deep into her eyes, he tucked the last gardenia in her hair, then cupped her face in his hands.

She thought he was going to kiss her. Although she tried to steel herself against the emotions that were swamping her, every nerve in her body was tingling with the need to be kissed.

"No," she whispered. She didn't know whether she'd meant it as an answer to his question or as a last-ditch effort to keep herself from tumbling into the magic spell he was weaving. Whatever she'd meant, it didn't seem to matter. With Hunter's hands on her face like that, tender and possessive and loving, nothing seemed to matter except the moment.

"I'm resurrecting a memory," he said.

She tried to pull away. "Hunter, don't."

"Yes." His thumbs caressed her lips. "Remember when we met, Mattie?"

"Please." Her eyes were huge as she struggled with her ambivalent emotions. She wanted to remember.

She wanted to recall the days of love and joy and innocence. She wanted to go backward in time until she could find her sweet teddy-bear man once more. But she was afraid. She was afraid of becoming vulnerable.

"Remember how it was, Mattie? Phillip had just bought the house next door. You'd come to spend your eighteenth summer with him. He was throwing a party for you." His voice mesmerized her, transported her back. "The gardenias were in bloom. Phillip had brought in a carrousel."

She remembered. . . .

The carrousel had been shipped in from Nashville. It was bright red and blue, with swan-shaped seats and wooden horses with rainbow-colored saddles. She'd been balanced precariously atop one of the horses, holding on to a dozen balloons with one hand and the carrousel pole with the other.

"Icarus used wings," someone said. She looked down and saw a man who was young and handsome and had the blackest eyes she'd ever seen. He seemed to have materialized out of thin air. "If you're planning to fly," he continued, "you'll need more than a handful of balloons."

She'd never seen a smile so devastating, and nearly fell off the horse.

"Careful, there." He put his hands on her bare legs to steady her. "I'd never forgive myself if you broke your neck first."

"First?" She thought his voice matched his smile, beguiling and sexy and altogether wonderful.

"Before I kiss you."

Her cheeks turned as pink as the ribbon holding back her hair. "Who are you?"

"You don't kiss strangers, huh? I'm glad, because I'm afraid I'm going to be the jealous type."

She tossed her head and tried to look haughty. "I

think you're the most audacious man I've ever met. Furthermore, you're trespassing."

"No. I'm paying a neighborly call. I'm Hunter Chadwick, from the house next door, and I can't wait to become better acquainted with my new neighbor. But you'll have to come down from that horse first."

"You're going to have a long wait. I happen to be hanging these balloons for a party, and I have no intention of coming down to get better acquainted with you. You're much too arrogant."

"Does that mean I have to come up?"

His smile almost undid her, but she managed to hide her own smile by catching her lower lip between her teeth. "Besides," she added, "you're much too old for me."

"I can see you're going to require a long courtship." He bent over and plucked a gardenia off a nearby bush. "First the flowers." He sprang on top of the carrousel horse beside hers and tucked the gardenia in her hair. "Then the candy." Hanging on to the carrousel pole with one hand, he reached into his pocket with the other and pulled out a lollipop. He peeled off the wrapper and unceremoniously plopped it into her mouth. "Next the family history. My father's Rafe Chadwick, a well-known criminal lawyer. My mother is a Langston, old money, can trace her roots back to Richard the Lionhearted. And there's not a single skeleton in our closet that you wouldn't be proud to claim as your uncle. As for me—I've left the dusty old legal tomes for more steadfast young men and have decided to devote myself to the making of toys. Toy-making will come second, of course."

She laughed. He was so endearing, she couldn't help herself. Taking the lollipop from her mouth, she asked, "What comes first?"

"This." He leaned over and kissed her cheek. "And this." Next he kissed her nose. "Then this." He captured her ripe berry lips in a kiss that made her toes curl. When he finally lifted his head, his black eyes blazed with undisguised desire. "It gets better all the time." He gently brushed a strand of red-gold hair from her cheek. "You never told me your name."

"Mattie Houston."

"This is going to be a summer to remember, Mattie Houston. . . .

And it had been. Mattie closed her eyes as the sweet pain of remembering swept over her. Hunter's hands on her face felt as right and wonderful as they had that long-ago summer. Around them, the music of the carrousels played on.

"First this, Mattie." He brushed her cheek with his lips. "Then this." Her nose came next, and then his mouth crushed down on hers. But it wasn't the sweet, innocent kiss of ten years ago. It was very adult, very expert, and very persuasive.

Unconsciously she wound her arms around his neck, and the sheet slid to her waist. He gathered her close as his tongue plundered her mouth. The erotic abrasion of his chest hair caused her nipples to tighten into dusky rose peaks. His hands caressed the warm silkiness of her back, and his mouth devoured hers with a wild need that left them breathless.

"It's been so long," he whispered against her lips. "Do you have any idea how I've missed you?"

Before she could answer, he lowered his head and took one of her taut nipples into his mouth. "Nectar for the gods." He pressed his face into her softness, his mouth and tongue wetting, circling, sucking, until Mattie was beyond words. Then he moved to the other breast, his murmured words betraying the wild delirium of his passion. "My sweet Mattie . . . perfection . . . enough to drive . . . a man . . . insane . . ." His mouth suckled until she was wet with desire. "Mattie, I need you."

He lifted his head, his eyes blazing into hers, and

she was lost. Lost in a forever dream of a love that wouldn't die. The music of the carrousels invaded her.

He lowered her to the bed and pushed the sheet away from her body. His eyes were glittering black star sapphires as he gazed at her. "You're even more beautiful than I remembered." Suddenly his weight was on top of her and his arms were around her, squeezing as if he never intended to let go. "Mattie, Mattie," he murmured into her hair. She felt the stunning size and heat of him through his cut-offs.

And she almost surrendered. She was tempted to answer that broken plea, tempted to give herself up to the joy that was flooding her soul and the need that was ripping through her body. But the small voice of reason finally pushed its way through the desire that fogged her brain and made itself heard. What she felt now was a mistake, a trick of fate. The man she truly desired didn't exist, had never really existed except in her youthful imagination. Ten years ago her Prince Charming had displayed feet of clay, and nothing had happened to change that.

One by one the carrousel music boxes wound down. The last notes of "The Way We Were" died away, leaving a sad stillness in the room.

Her arms loosened and her body went slack. She couldn't bring herself to make love with Hunter, not even to seek vengeance. She'd almost surrendered because of love remembered. She'd come so close, she was shaken. Her game of revenge was dangerous, more dangerous than she'd ever imagined. At that moment she fully understood the risks she was taking. Hunter was a practiced lover, a spellbinding man. If she weren't very careful, she'd find herself believing that she could fall in love with him again.

No, she decided. This was neither the time nor the place to finish the game she'd started. Another day, perhaps, after she'd gotten a better perspective.

Hunter immediately sensed the change in her. Lifting his head, he gazed into her eyes. "Mattie?"

"No, Hunter. Get up."

A fleeting look of pain crossed his face. Then he smiled. "Not before breakfast, huh?"

"No. Not before breakfast." She hid her vulnerability behind a brittle facade. Play the game, she told herself. Dangle the bait, pull back, make him crazy, then break his heart. As she looked up at him she wondered why she wasn't gloating over her success.

"Breakfast before pleasure, then," he said. "You always did have the appetite of a stevedore." He sat up and reached for the breakfast tray. Shoving the gardenias aside, he placed it on the bed between them.

"Breakfast *instead* of pleasure." She reached over and patted his face. "For today, at least. I don't intend to keep a randy man like you waiting forever." She gave him the look of sizzling promise that had caused more than one sheik to swear off harems.

Two days ago Hunter would have reveled in that look, but today it made him angry and somewhat sad. He wanted to grab her and shout, "Dammit, Mattie! Don't! Don't play the flirt with me." Instead he smiled ruefully. What had he expected? He wanted her anyway. As he poured the coffee, he decided that the tricks of fate weren't always easy to live with.

"Coffee's hot, Mattie." He handed her a cup. "And so am I. I'd advise you not to jiggle."

"I'll leave jiggling to the likes of Gwendolyn. I writhe."

The images that remark created made Hunter want to smash his fist into the wall. "No doubt."

She tucked the sheet securely over her breasts, and sipped her coffee. "Is it your habit to shower your women with flowers before breakfast?" She nodded toward the gardenias, which were being crushed against the mattress.

He grinned. "Jealous, Mattie?"

"No. Just curious. It's been so long. I'd like to learn your mating habits, so I'll know what to expect next time."

"You used to like surprises."

"I don't anymore. The last surprise I had—" She stopped in mid-sentence. She'd almost confessed to Hunter, her enemy, that the last surprise she'd had, had almost destroyed her. That would never do. She tossed her head and laughed. "The last surprise I had cost me a small fortune. I'd taken Pierre's car to the Champs de Mars. I didn't know the brakes were bad. I ran over two merry-go-rounds and three puppet booths and damn near hit the Eiffel Tower before I could stop."

"You could have been killed. What's the matter with that fool? Why didn't he tell you his brakes weren't working?"

"He didn't know I'd borrowed the car. There'd been a party at his chateau. I just suddenly decided to leave." She deliberately left out all the best parts of the story— how Pierre had not been satisfied with heated kisses and empty promises, how he'd been more insistent than the rest, how he'd nearly ripped her dress off her before she'd pushed him into the fountain.

She looked at Hunter over the rim of her cup. "If you only knew," she said silently, "what I've gone through trying to forget you."

Hunter balled his hands into fists. He hated them all. Pierre and the ones whose names he didn't know. He hated all of Mattie's lovers. He hated them so fiercely, it scared him. Forcing himself to calm down, he reached across the crushed gardenias and touched her cheek. "I'll see to it that you never get another sudden urge to leave me, Mattie."

She meant to say something bright and frivolous. She meant to be sophisticated and brittle and wordly-wise.

Instead she whispered, "Another?"

"Yes." He caressed her face. "Why did you go?"

"Not again, Hunter. Don't ask me again."

"I intend to find out, you know."

"Why?"

He looked deep into her eyes. Now was not the time to say he was falling in love with her, he decided. Too much had happened between them. If he intended to win Mattie—and he did—he'd have to take it one step at a time.

"Call it stubbornness," he said. "Call it ego. A man doesn't like to think he's been jilted for no reason at all."

She sucked in her breath. She had a sudden vision of her mother's beautiful, tear-stained face. All her love for her mother and her rage at Hunter surfaced. "No reason at all!" she shouted.

Her violent reaction startled Hunter. He tightened his hold. "What in hell happened ten years ago, Mattie?"

His innocent act almost fooled her. She almost confronted him with the ugly truth—as if he didn't already know. Instead she brushed his hand away. At least his statement had served some purpose. It had restored her sanity. She fought for and gained the control she needed.

"Consider yourself forewarned, Hunter. I don't need any reason to walk away. I jilt men like you every day just for the fun of it."

"Not this time, Mattie." He handed her a piece of toast. "Eat your breakfast. You're going to need your strength."

Then he walked out of the room.

Mattie looked thoughtfully at the closed door. "You don't scare me, Hunter Chadwick." She nibbled a small piece of toast, then took a big bite, then spread on the strawberry jam. She ate everything on her tray except the coffeepot. Getting the best of Hunter was going to take all the strength she could muster.

Two days later Hunter sat in Phillip Houston's study. He'd made sure Mattie wasn't home. He'd seen her leave thirty minutes before with another of those Neanderthal men she seemed to prefer.

"I'll come right to the point, Mr. Houston. I've never stopped loving your granddaughter."

"Took you a hell of a long time finding it out, didn't it?" Phillip sat staunchly behind his massive desk, keeping the interview on a formal level. He wasn't going to make it easy for Hunter, he decided. Much as he liked the boy, he was going to make damn sure he didn't hurt Mattie again.

"Ten years *is* a long time," Hunter said. "I don't blame you for being suspicious. I suppose the ignorance and foolish pride of youth kept me from going after her sooner."

To Hunter's surprise, Phillip laughed. "Ignorance and foolish pride are not limited to the young. I've seen some old coots who've cornered the market on those commodities. Your Uncle Mickey, for one. And from time to time I've been guilty myself. Not often, mind you. But often enough to let me know I'm not nearly as perfect as I'd like to believe."

Hunter was eager to get on with his pursuit of the past, but he could see that Phillip was enjoying expounding on the topic. He'd already waited ten years, and figured a few more minutes wouldn't kill him. "You've always impressed me," he said. "And I consider Uncle Mickey as nearly perfect as any person I know."

"Get him to tell you about Mrs. Cleary sometime. Damn foolish business, if I ever heard it. Told him so at the time, but you know Mickey. Stubborn as a mule."

Hunter laughed. "Sometimes he can be. Dad always says it's a Langston family trait."

"I'll bet Eleanor doesn't take that sitting down. A regular spitfire, your mom is. Always did admire her. I used to wish William had exercised as much judgment as Rafe Chadwick in choosing a wife." Phillip looked off into space. "Yessir, that Eleanor is one helluva fine woman."

"Thank you. The next time I see her, I'll tell her you said so."

"Where are Rafe and Eleanor?"

"They're spending the summer at their Lake Tahoe place."

"Beautiful country. Wouldn't mind being there myself. Of course, Mrs. Cleary and that granddaughter of mine think I'm getting too old to travel." He stood up and executed a perfect roundhouse kick. "Did you see that, boy? Does that look like an old man to you?"

"A man of thirty-five would be proud of that karate kick." Hunter relaxed in his chair. It looked as if this interview was going to take a long time.

Phillip sat back down and leaned forward across his desk. "What do you plan to do about it?"

"Sir?"

"My granddaughter. You said you loved her. What do you plan to do about it?"

"I plan to marry her."

"Has she said yes?"

"She doesn't know it yet. "

"I guess I don't understand these newfangled courtships. Mattie off over yonder and you in Dallas. Waiting ten years. In my day, love wasn't so complicated."

"Ours is more complicated than most. You see, I don't even know why Mattie left me in the first place. That's one of the reasons I'm here. I want to find out."

Phillip propped his elbows on his desk and put his fingertips together. "I've always wondered about that myself."

So not even Phillip knew, Hunter thought. He could almost taste the bitterness of his disappointment.

"Did anything unusual happen the day she returned my ring?" he asked.

"Not that I recall. Let me see, now. . . . " Phillip's fingers tapped lightly together as he looked backward in time. "That was the same week her mother came. William stayed in London on business. I remember how happy Mattie was. She showed her mother the ring that night at dinner. I didn't notice anything unusual."

"Was Victoria pleased? Mattie was only eighteen."

Hunter was not the son of a famous lawyer for nothing. In his desperation, he'd try anything, even questioning Phillip like a trial attorney.

"Nothing Mattie ever did pleased her." Phillip's lips were white with anger. "She was a self-centered, egotistical woman who cared about nothing except keeping lines off that famous face of hers and seeing how many men she could flaunt in front of William." His face became haggard as he remembered the humiliation his son had suffered. "Poor William. He always made excuses for her. He said she never actually did anything with the men, that she just kept them around to affirm her beauty. I knew better. If he'd ever admitted the truth to himself, I think it would have killed him."

"I'm sorry. I didn't mean to dredge up painful memories."

Phillip held up a steady hand. "That's all right. From time to time I let the bitterness out. Keeps it from poisoning the system."

"I guess that's what I'm trying to do: decipher the bitterness that's still between Mattie and me." He stood up to leave. "Thank you for being so frank with me."

"Wait. It seems there was more . . . if I can just remember it." Phillip grinned. "Sometimes the body's easier to keep in shape than the mind."

Hunter sat back down.

"I remember," Phillip continued. "A couple of days after Victoria got home, you and Mattie went on a picnic. Mattie came back laughing, all aglow with sunshine and smiles. . . ."

Phillip paused. Hunter remembered that day. Mattie had been exuberant, joyful . . . and especially loving. And the next day, she'd returned his ring.

"It was late at night," Phillip continued. "I could hear them talking."

Hunter tensed, leaned forward. "Who?"

"Victoria and Mattie. The following day, they left to join William in London."

"After she'd returned my ring," Hunter said grimly. "What in the hell did Victoria say to her?"

"I used to wonder that myself. But neither of them ever mentioned it, and I respected their privacy. Especially Mattie's."

Hunter stood up and shook Phillip's hand. "Thank you. You've given me something to go on."

"I'm not sure she ever got over you, boy. I've never believed that wild lifestyle of hers was anything more than a cover-up. Mattie would deny it with her last breath, but deep down she's a sweet girl." He clapped his hand on Hunter's shoulder. "I don't want to see her hurt again."

"I can promise you one thing, Mr. Houston. I'll never hurt Mattie."

Phillip grinned. "Call me Papa."

Six

It took Mattie three days to get over her encounter with Hunter. First she tried to reduce his appeal by going out with other men. Chuck proved to be the best anti-dote. He had nothing on his mind except impressing her with the number of men he'd knocked out in the boxing ring and flexing his muscles for her. "Feel that," he'd say. "This sucker packs a punch. Nobody will mess around with you as long as Chuck ("the Gorilla") Bucy is with you." He was as uncomplicated as popcorn— and exactly what she needed in order to get her life back into perspective.

But the cure was only temporary.

Next she sought refuge in her favorite pastime—poker. Papa Houston was pressed into duty as her partner.

"Five-card stud, Papa. Ante up." Mattie handled the cards like an expert, shuffling, fanning, cutting with the precision of a professional.

"I don't know why I agreed to play with you," Papa grumbled. "You always cheat."

Mattie laughed. She knew he loved cards. "You always say that, because you never win." She quickly dealt them two cards each, one face up.

Papa's face card was a king of spades. He lifted the

edge of his other card and tried to keep the smile off his face. He was holding a pair of kings and Mattie had a four of hearts showing. He could already taste the victory. Deliberately, he kept his first bid low, to throw his granddaughter off track.

"I'll bet twenty," he said.

"Call." She dealt two more cards, another king to Papa and a jack to herself. Her face was inscrutable. She played cards the way she did everything else, wholeheartedly and with total concentration. For the first time in three days, Hunter was forgotten.

"Get ready to lose this one, granddaughter."

"You're supposed to play with a poker face."

"The game's no fun if you can't gloat over your winning hand."

"You haven't won yet, Papa."

The bidding became lively as the last two rounds of cards went down. There was laughter and lots of friendly gibing. Both the Houstons loved games and delighted in competition. Besides that, they were fiercely proud of each other, Mattie loved Papa's quick mind and youthful spirit. He loved her vitality and wit and charm.

After the last card was down and the last bid made, Papa fanned his cards on the table.

"Three kings," he announced grandly.

Mattie spread her cards, three fours and two jacks. "Full house. I won, Papa."

His eyes sparkled with humor. "I taught you everything you know."

"You certainly did. That's what I tell them when I go to Monte Carlo."

"I bet they're impressed."

Mattie smiled at her dear Papa. There was nothing shy and retiring about him, she thought. She loved that boldness, that arrogance. Suddenly Hunter came to her mind. He was so like Papa in that way.

"They are impressed." She stood up and kissed his cheek. "I have to dress for rehearsal now."

"We'll have a rematch later. Wow 'em Mattie."

"I intend to."

As she climbed the stairs, Hunter was very much on her mind. Somehow he had managed to warp her thinking. He kept slipping out of his role of deceiver and becoming the rakish, lovable man she'd first known. The kisses that were intended to be a means of retaliation kept turning into exchanges of heated passion. During the last three days, she'd been so confused, she wasn't sure who was the pursuer and who the pursued. The game she'd started out to play wasn't her game anymore. Hunter kept making it his.

Not today, she decided as she pinned her hair into a careless topknot and zipped herself into a baby-blue jump suit. It was slit nearly to her navel in front and all the way to her waist in the back. And it was calculated to drive Hunter crazy.

She left the house, climbed into her car, and headed for the rehearsal hall. Thank goodness she hadn't been required to attend for the last three days. It had taken her that long to prepare herself for seeing Hunter again. She kept conjuring up his string of other women in order to forget the way his kisses made her feel. Even now he entered her mind with such sexual force, she had to struggle to control her emotions.

She was so busy thinking about Hunter, she almost passed the rehearsal hall. Her tires squealed as she braked and swerved sharply into the parking lot. She zoomed haphazardly between the parked cars and brought her Porsche to a rubber-burning stop mere inches from Hunter's Maserati.

He was suddenly beside her car, flinging open her door. "No wonder you wrecked everything in the Champs de Mars," he said. Smiling, he propped his arms on top of her car and leaned close to her face. "What is it about you, Mattie, that excites the hell out of me?"

"Overactive hormones." She smiled sweetly up at him.

He roared with laughter. When his mirth died, he cocked an eyebrow at her and drawled, "Whose? Yours or mine?"

"Both." She started to get out of her car, but he blocked her exit. "You're standing in my way."

"No, I'm not. I'm in exactly the right spot."

"For what?"

"Kidnapping." He reached inside the car and took her keys. "You won't be needing these today."

"Are you crazy?"

"No. Just oversexed."

Still blocking her doorway, he half turned, and motioned toward his car. A grinning young man with freckles and a cowlick emerged from the Maserati.

"Jimmy, take Miss Houston's car home." Hunter dropped the keys into Jimmy's outstretched hand, then bent down and scooped Mattie out of the front seat. Holding her tightly, he strolled around to the driver's side of his car and watched as his gardener, handyman, and sometime chauffeur drove off in Mattie's car.

She glared up at him. This wasn't at all the way things were supposed to work out today, she thought. She'd meant to be completely in charge. "Put me down, you pirate."

"Certainly not. I intend to sweep you off your feet, Mattie. How am I doing so far?"

She thought he was doing remarkably well, but she wasn't about to say so. "You're batting zero."

"Maybe this will help."

He leaned down and circled his tongue around her nipple. It betrayed her by pushing against the wet fabric. The amber light leaped into his eyes as he gazed at her.

"Did it?" he asked.

"You're the most arrogant, conceited man in Dallas."

He laughed. "I probably am." Still holding her, he opened his car door, then scooted her carefully around the steering wheel and arranged her on the front seat. With his face only inches from hers, he crooned. "That's all right, love. You don't have to answer my question. Your body already did."

He settled in the driver's seat and started the car.

"Don't you dare start this car, you conceited stud," she said. "You can't just take me off like this."

He backed expertly out of the parking lot. "I already did, Mattie."

Sometimes Mattie lost track of how she was supposed to be feeling about Hunter, but she never lost track of how she felt about music. She was first and foremost a professional.

"We'll miss rehearsal," she said.

"Jo Ann knows we won't be there." He was maddeningly silent as he left the freeway and turned toward downtown Dallas. Finally he glanced toward her. "I told Jo Ann the star of the show had begged me to take her on a picnic today, and naturally she agreed that we should both do everything in our power to keep the star happy."

He was so like the outrageous Hunter she'd once loved, that she had to bite her tongue to keep from smiling. Remembered summer days of the wind in her hair and Hunter at her side invaded her, and she was happy.

"You're a wicked, devious, presumptuous, skirt-chasing playboy." She was choking back laughter the entire time she said all those things. She used to love his spontaneity. And his wickedness. As for the rest of her accusations . . . she just wouldn't think too seriously about all that today. She was having too much fun.

"You left out one," he said.

"What?"

"Desirable."

"Conceited."

"But cute." He reached over and rubbed her leg. "How did you ever get along without me, Mattie?"

The question touched an old wound. She'd gotten along without him in stages that ranged from total despair to flickering hope to stubborn denial. She turned her face to the window when she answered him. "The same way you got along without me, Hunter." Let him make whatever he wanted of it, she decided.

"All that's behind us now," he said.

She couldn't study his face without being obvious, so she didn't know whether or not he was teasing.

"Where are we going?" she asked.

"To the stars. We may never come back."

"That's a nice line, Hunter. Do you use it on all your women?"

He chuckled. "Let's make a deal. For today I'll forget all your other men if you'll forget all my other women."

"That's going to be hard, especially the Russian prince."

"I'll make you forget." He swerved over a curb, slammed on the brakes, and stopped so hard, her teeth were jolted together.

"Hunter! You're parked on a sidewalk."

"What's the matter, Mattie?" He slid over and took her into his arms. "I thought you liked to live dangerously," he said, and kissed her with such savage force, she couldn't have replied if she'd wanted to.

She had a fleeting thought that nothing seemed to be going the way she'd planned today. Then she gave herself up to the delicious feelings that were storming through her body. She was jazz, insistent and throbbing. She was summer song, hot and pulsing. And while his mouth savaged hers, she was Hunter's woman.

She made a small sound that was half sigh, half moan as she circled his neck with her arms and laced her fingers through his wild hair. It came alive under her fingers, winding itself around them, thick and crisp and vital, as vital as the man whose lips sought to blot out their past.

"We could scandalize Dallas," he murmured.

Once again she couldn't reply, for the scorching heat of his tongue filled her mouth, plying fiercely, urgently, until she was as limp as the damp hair that clung to the back of her neck.

Pedestrians did a double take at the sight of a car on

the sidewalk. Most of them eased around it, figuring it was none of their business what the foolish rich did with their expensive cars. They gave no more than a passing glance to the two people glued together on the front seat.

However, one woman who believed in speaking her mind wherever she happened to be tapped smartly on the driver's window with her walking stick. Mattie and Hunter ignored her, being occupied with the fire that blazed between them.

The fearless woman pressed her face to the window, the better to determine exactly what was going on. What she saw made her wish she were young again.

"Young man," she called. When she received no reply, she called louder. "Young man."

Hunter looked up at the wrinkled old face pressed against his window. Still holding Mattie close, he pressed a button and eased the window down. "Anything I can do for you?" he asked as politely as if he had been at a Sunday-school picnic.

The elderly woman stuck her head through the window. "You can call me the next time you plan to put on another show. The name's Letitia Hart, and I approve. Not enough romance in today's world."

"I completely agree." Hunter smiled first at the woman, then at Mattie. "Don't you, darling?"

Mattie's heart was bumping so hard against her rib cage, she could barely think, let alone speak. "Ummm," she said.

Hunter grinned. "My wife's a woman of few words. I like it that way. Gives me more time to concentrate on the important things."

"Like romance." Letitia nodded. "The world needs more men like you." She backed her head out of the car. "Carry on."

"I intend to." He pressed the button, and the window whirred back up. "Nice woman, that Letitia. Now." His gaze swept over Mattie. "Where were we?"

Mattie had almost recovered. She decided to take

control of the situation. "I was very close to ripping your clothes off and having my way with you, Hunter." She gave him a teasing smile.

"I'll help you, Mattie. What do you want to start with? My shirt?" He made a move to strip it over his head.

She put her hand on his. "You've proved your point, whatever it is. Get this car off the sidewalk."

Grinning, he put the car into gear and backed into the street. "The point, dear Mattie, is that I intend to have you. No matter what you say, no matter what you do, you're going to be mine."

She supposed she should be happy about that. Wasn't that a part of her plan? To make Hunter want her? Then why the hell wasn't she gloating? What was the matter with her?

She forced herself to continue the game. "Then I have to warn you, Hunter. I don't like more than two in a bed."

He grinned. "Does that mean I have to give up my other women?"

"Definitely. I don't like to share."

"Neither do I."

The intensity of his voice startled her. She turned to study his face. His expression was almost stern. But, of course, that was because he was concentrating on the traffic. It had nothing whatever to do with what he'd said. He was playing a game too. Funny, she had to keep reminding herself of that.

Hunter turned into the parking lot of Chadwick Toys and stopped the car beside one of the storage warehouses.

"This is it, Mattie. Our destination."

"This is your company, Hunter?" Her excitement was genuine as she looked at the vast toy-manufacturing complex. "I've always wanted to see it."

He smiled a secret smile. In moments when we least expect it, the truth slips out, he thought. And that particular truth made him extremely happy. It meant that Mattie had thought of him through the years. It meant that a part of her still cared. He could build on that.

In typical Hunter fashion, he forged straight ahead. "Then you shall see it. I'll give you the executive tour. I want you to see exactly how the father of your future children makes his living."

He was out the door and striding around to her side of the car before she could reply. First her face went red hot. Then it turned white. She didn't like this game, she decided. How many times in the last ten years had she thought of the waste? How many times had she imagined the children they would have had? A deep ache started inside her, and she was forlorn, Rachel mourning for her children.

Hunter opened the car door and took her hand. "Come, beautiful princess of jazz. Let me show you your future kingdom."

She wanted to scream, "Stop it." She wanted to bang her fists against his chest and yell that this wasn't part of the game. Talk of children and a future meant falling in love. Didn't Hunter know that was an impossible dream?

"Your hand is cold, Mattie." He smiled down at her. "Does that mean your heart is warm?"

"I have no heart, Hunter. Didn't you know that?" Her smile was forced, her voice brittle.

"Then you've come to the right place. Chadwick Toys has its own resident wizard. He can give you a new heart."

"Who is this resident wizard?"

"Me."

He pushed open the door to his vast toy warehouse. Red wagons and fire engines and tricycles and dolls and wooden ponies and teddy bears were lined in neat rows like ranks of miniature soldiers ready for battle.

Mattie felt as if she had entered the magic world of childhood. Seeing all the toys, all the symbols of childhood dreams, made her misty-eyed.

She looked at Hunter. "It's your dream come true," she said softly.

"Only part of it." He gently brushed a stray curl away from her cheek. "I specialize in making dreams come true, Mattie. And I intend to complete my dream. All of it."

"Hunter. Don't."

"You remember the dream, don't you, Mattie?"

"Yes." Her voice was barely a whisper. She remembered. . . .

They'd gone on a picnic. It was nearing the end of the summer. Both were already feeling the impending doom of her leaving.

Hunter took two huge picnic hampers from the trunk of his Thunderbird, and she laughed as he pretended to struggle across the beach. "We'll never eat all that."

He put the baskets down, then opened one and took out a teddy-bear puppet. Sticking his hand inside and working the mouth, he said in his best teddy-bear voice, "I certainly hope not. People don't eat bears; bears eat people." Then he wrapped Mattie in his arms. "Starting with you."

His lips tasted of sun and wind and summer. She clung to the solid strength of him, never wanting to let go. His hands moved over her body, tracing the familiar lines of her back, the curve of her buttocks, the lithe firmness of her thighs. She felt the soft warmth of the teddy bear's fur as Hunter memorized her.

"Marry me, Mattie," he said against her lips.

Joy leaped within her. She pulled back and looked into his face. "I'm only eighteen, Hunter. I'd always planned to finish my music studies before I married."

"That was before you met me." He pulled her down on the sand and tucked her securely against his body. "We'll make it work, Mattie. I know how important music is to you. But I also know that you love me."

"I do."

"You can have both. Let's don't wait, Mattie. Let's make our dreams come true together."

She pressed her head against his chest, reassured by the steady drumming of his heart. Being with Hunter somehow made everything seem right. "Tell me how it'll be, Hunter. Spin those magic dreams again."

He lifted her hand and placed a lingering kiss on her palm. "I'll make toys and you'll make music . . . and together we'll make magic. You'll be the best jazz musician in America and I'll be the biggest toy manufacturer. My toys will fulfill the dream of every kid in America, including our own." He twined her fingers with his. "Our love is so special, Mattie, that we'll want to share it. We'll have children, lots of them. And we'll be so happy we'll be the envy of everybody in Dallas."

She rolled over on top of him. "I'll marry you."

He laughed. "You forgot to say yes."

"Yes, yes, yes, yes, yes . . ."

. . . Yes, she remembered, and the memory ripped a hole in her heart.

"I'm going to have it all, Mattie."

His face was as implacable as time. Before she could reply, Hunter changed from formidable to playful.

"Come on, Mattie. Let's have fun." He grabbed her hand and pulled her down the aisle of toys. "We'll need this." He plucked a teddy bear off the shelf and dropped it into her arms. "And this . . . and this . . . and this . . . and this." He piled her arms with teddy bears as he talked. "What's a picnic without teddy bears?"

He whisked her to the warehouse roof by way of an old-fashioned, creaky elevator. As she hugged the bears close she wondered if he treated all his women to these impulsive picnics. The thought made her jealous, and then she was miffed at herself for even caring.

Hunter escorted her through the door and onto the sunlit roof. A table for two was set with linen and crystal and silver, a three-piece combo was playing the best jazz west of the Mississippi, and hundreds of teddy bears were already arranged around the rooftop, seated on chairs and in corners, as if they'd come especially for the party.

"You call this a picnic?" Mattie asked.

"Yes. Fit for a princess. How do you like it so far?"

She liked it. In fact, she loved it. But she'd be damned if she'd tell him so.

"Hunter, if this is another one of your schemes to make me remember what we once had, forget it."

"Never fear, Mattie. These teddy bears don't even eat people." He plucked one from her arms and rubbed it against her cheek. "See?"

She smiled. "He took a nibble."

"I don't blame him." He took all the bears and put them on the floor. "Just for today, let's forget the past. Let's act as if there's nothing between us except mutual attraction."

"I'm not attracted—"

"Yes, you are." He pressed a finger against her lips. "Just you and me, with the wind in our hair and the sun on our faces." He took her into his arms. "Let's dance."

She smoothly followed his lead. "Why not? The music is very good. Who are they?"

"Rod and Herman and Axel Franklin, good friends of mine." He pulled her a bit closer. "I'd forgotten how well you dance."

"I thought you said no memories."

"Right. What do you have for breakfast, Mattie? Do you eat apples with the peelings or without? What do you do for exercise? Do you read murder mysteries? Who's your favorite man?" He winked. "The answer to that one is Hunter Chadwick."

She tipped back her head and laughed. "Cereal and fruit. With. Swimming and hiking. No. And not you."

"You lie." He held her so tightly, she could feel every muscle in his body.

"I always lie when I'm hungry."

"Then let's eat."

They sat at the table and shared fruit and cheese and wine and croissants so flaky that bits of crust clung to their lips. With the music playing and the sun shining down on them, they were nothing more than two handsome people, intensely attracted to each other. The past faded and the games they'd been playing were forgotten. They laughed and talked and perfectly imitated two people falling in love.

"Hey, save some cheese for me, Hunter. You must be part mouse."

"I am. Are you part cat?"

"Why?"

"I'm waiting for a beautiful, sleek cat to gobble me up."

"That's me. Mattie the cat. Meow."

"When are you going to eat me?"

"As soon as I jump over the moon."

"That's a cow that jumped over the moon, Mattie. Not a cat."

"Are you calling me a cow? I'm udderly insulted."

"You're also utterly gorgeous and desirable and delicious. I'm thinking of having you for dessert."

"You told me these bears don't eat people."

"Are you calling me a bear?"

"Yes. You're my sweet teddy-bear man."

Mattie was having so much fun, she didn't notice her slip of the tongue.

But Hunter did. He was so thrilled, he had to restrain himself from leaping across the table and kissing her until they were both limp. There was hope, he thought. After all that had happened between them, there was still hope.

He smiled a secret smile and continued romancing his Mattie.

Mattie propped the teddy bear on her bedside table. He had black button eyes and plush brown fur and was soft and cuddly. Hunter had given her the bear as a memento of the picnic, and she'd named him Henry.

"Well, Henry," she said as she undressed, "I wish you could talk. Maybe you could tell me about this enigmatic man called Hunter Chadwick. How can he be so damned arrogant and passionate one minute and so gentle and likable the next? He never even tried to kiss me again after we went into that warehouse. Except for that peck on the cheek when he brought me home. Does that make sense to you?"

She covered her naked perfection with a filmy peignoir and stood smiling at the bear. "Today, Henry, I almost forgave him. He was so charming, I came close to burying the past. I almost forgot about his harem."

She picked up the bear and stroked his fur. "You're a good listener. Has anybody ever told you that?" She cuddled the teddy bear against her cheek. "Do you know how hard I've tried to forget that man? I wanted so desperately to fall in love that I've chased half the men in Europe. The papers report it the other way around, of course." She snuggled her nose into Henry's soft tummy. "Nobody knows that but you and Papa. Don't tell a soul, cuddly old teddy bear." She placed Henry back on the chair. "Today I felt as if I were falling in love again. That's totally impossible."

She began to pace, punctuating her words with dramatic, sweeping gestures. "They say love is blind. It must be crazy, too. I have no intention of falling in love with the man who betrayed me. Besides that, how could I ever trust a man who has keys to half the bedrooms in Dallas? I'll just have to forget today. That's all. I'm going to accept it as a pleasant interlude. Tomorrow I'll analyze all this."

"Good night, Henry."

She left her bedroom and went into the music room. The piano gleamed a rich mahogany in the moonlight. She didn't even bother to turn on the lights. Her hands knew the ivories as intimately as a woman knows her lover. She sat on the piano bench and began to play, leaning into the music, having an affair with the keyboard.

And the song she played was "Summer Wind."

Hunter heard the song. He stood on his patio listening until the last note had died away. Then he went inside. He walked straight to his Uncle Mickey's room and tapped on the door.

"Come in," Uncle Mickey said. "I've been expecting you."

Uncle Mickey was wearing peppermint-striped pajamas. He was tall and lean and bony, and he looked like a candy cane.

Hunter sprawled in an old stuffed chair. Its upholstery was worn and its cushions sagged, but it had the familiar fit and comfort of a favorite pair of bedroom slippers. And it was a bone of contention between Hunter's mother and her uncle. Hunter rubbed his hand across the worn arm and smiled. His mother had tried everything, including threats to cart the old chair off and throw it into Ray Hubbard Lake. But Uncle Mickey had remained staunch, declaring that a man's bedroom should be sacred, and untouched by meddling nieces.

"I heard you had a special pea tarty at the warehouse today," Uncle Mickey said. "I knew you'd have things to tell me."

"It's working, Uncle Mickey. Mattie's falling in love with me."

Uncle Mickey smiled. "Any woman in her right mind would."

"She hasn't changed all that much, you know. She's still spontaneous and spirited and quick to laugh. I can almost believe she's the same Mattie Houston."

"But she's not, Hunter. Don't make the mistake of building your love on a dream."

Hunter ran his hands through his hair. "I know.

She's not really the same. But, hell, neither am I. We've both been around."

"Take my advice. Forget all that, Hunter. Take what you have now, who you are now, and go from there."

"You give great advice, Uncle Mickey. Especially for an inexperienced old bachelor." He gave his uncle a sly grin.

"Is that a leading statement?"

"Yes. Tell me about Mrs. Cleary."

"Who told you?"

"Phillip Houston."

Uncle Mickey crossed his bony knees and began his story. "I fell in love with Janet many years ago. We had an affair. Like most young people in love, we made all the plans, dreamed all the dreams. Then the war came along. I was reported missing in action. When I got home, she'd married Herbert Cleary. I put her out of my mind, lost track of her until she became Phillip Houston's housekeeper. That was a long time before Phillip moved next door. He and I go way back, you know."

Hunter knew. His uncle and Phillip had formed a fast friendship when they were college roommates. He'd often heard stories of their escapades.

"Anyway," Uncle Mickey continued, "seeing Janet again after all those years . . . I knew the spark was still there. She knew it too. We tried to deny it. We started up again, excusing our actions by telling ourselves that she deserved what little clandestine pleasure we could find. Her marriage was bad. Herbert was mean to her, mental cruelty. I don't know what would have happened if Herbert hadn't gotten sick. He became an invalid. We broke off the affair."

"Herbert Cleary's been dead for years, hasn't he? Why didn't the two of you get back together?"

"Guilt. We both felt guilty, as if we'd been the cause of Herbert's illness."

"That's foolish."

"That's what Phillip said. But we waited too long to

America's most popular, most compelling romance novels...

Here, at last...love stories that really involve you! Fresh, finely crafted novels with story lines so believable you'll feel you're actually living them! Characters you can relate to...exciting places to visit...unexpected plot twists...all in all, exciting romances that satisfy your mind and delight your heart.

Detach and mail this postage-paid card today!

Now you can be sure you'll never, ever miss a single Loveswept title by enrolling in our special reader's home delivery service. A service that will bring all four new Loveswept romances published every month into your home—and deliver them to you before they appear in the bookstores!

Examine 4 Loveswept Novels for

15 days FREE!

(SEE OTHER SIDE FOR DETAILS)

find that out. The guilt changed both of us. I disappeared into my world of toys, and Janet suppressed all her sexuality under starched aprons and starched attitudes."

"She's just next door. If you still love her, go after her."

Uncle Mickey smiled. "I guess it's never too late for love, but I'm used to the idea of being too old."

"I don't ever intend to be too old for love. I'll still be chasing Mattie when I'm ninety-five, even if I have to do it in a wheel chair." Hunter laughed at the idea. "It might be fun. I might even try it before I'm ninety-five."

Suddenly he turned serious. "All that's not why I came up here, Uncle Mickey. I've got to find out why Mattie left me ten years ago. All I know is that it happened after Victoria came to Dallas. Every time I ask Mattie about it, she becomes furious. Somehow I think Victoria is tied into it. Did you see her at all that summer?"

"Once. No . . ." He paused thoughtfully. "Twice. The first time, I'd gone over to play dominoes with Phillip. Victoria was back, more beautiful than ever. And cold . . . That woman had ice water in her veins. I don't think she even had a heart."

"I guess you knew her before I met Mattie."

"Yes. I'd seen her on several occasions—at her wedding, right after Mattie was born, and two or three times when she'd fly into Dallas and drop Mattie on Phillip's doorstep. She never enjoyed a conversation unless it was about herself, and as far as I could tell, she was never interested in anything except preserving her face and body. And collecting men. She kept herself surrounded by young studs. I think she believed they'd keep her from growing old."

"I never saw her as anything except a beautiful, charming woman."

Uncle Mickey snorted. "Every beautiful woman is charming when you're only twenty-six. Besides, you were seeing Mattie's mother through the eyes of love."

"You mentioned another time."

"What?"

Hunter smiled indulgently. In the way of creative people, his uncle Mickey was absentminded. Of course, Hunter reasoned, old age could be a factor, but it would be a very small one in this case. Both Uncle Mickey and Phillip Houston kept alert by being interested in the world around them.

"You said you saw Victoria twice that summer," Hunter prompted.

"Oh, yes. She'd asked if she could use your hot tub. One day while you and Mattie were gone, she called and said she wanted to come over. Said she had a couple of friends she wanted to bring. Naturally, I said yes. They were both men. One of them was young and good-looking. Had black hair like you. The other didn't look like Victoria's type at all. Sort of weather-beaten and dried-up-looking. He was carrying a bunch of equipment."

"What sort of equipment?"

"I didn't pay that much attention. I was on my way to play golf with Phillip. I just sort of waved and passed on by."

"Would Victoria have known that you and Phillip would be playing golf?"

"Could be. It was no secret. As a matter of fact, we might even have planned it the day I went over to play dominoes. Victoria was in and out that day. Restless-seeming."

Hunter made a steeple of his fingers while he digested these latest bits of information. He didn't have much to go on, but what he did have was beginning to make a very ugly picture—a beautiful, selfish woman who didn't want to grow old, who was possibly jealous of her daughter's youth and loveliness, a woman who liked young men. Could she have wanted him for herself? Why? She was a famous high-fashion model. Surely she could have had her pick of men. Apparently did, from what Uncle Mickey had said. And if she'd wanted to break up him and Mattie for that reason, why hadn't she made a play for him, especially after Mattie had returned the ring? He remembered his brief meetings with Victoria. She'd been nothing but pleasant to him. The puzzle pieces weren't fitting together right.

He saw Uncle Mickey attempt to stifle a yawn.

"I've kept you up late. I'm sorry, Uncle Mickey."

"It's my bedtime." He turned back the covers and winked at his great-nephew. "You've given me something to dream about. Yessir, in her day that Janet was something. A lovely body, that woman had. And a farming chase. Yessir, a farming chase." Uncle Mickey climbed into bed. "Good night, Hunter."

"Good night, Uncle Mickey. And thanks."

Hunter went to his room, but was too restless to go to bed. Walking to his window, he looked toward Mattie's house. There was still a light in her bedroom window.

He picked up his phone and dialed her number.

"Hello."

"Mattie. This is your teddy-bear man."

"Hunter!" He heard the smile in her voice, caught the excited lilt. Roses bloomed in his soul.

"Is Henry being a suitable stand-in?"

"For what?"

"For me."

She laughed. "He's sitting over there in a chair, like a proper gentleman."

"I'm going to fire that bear. He's supposed to be holding your hand and whispering sweet promises to fill all the empty places in your life."

She hesitated, then spoke with false cheerfulness. "How do you know I have empty places?"

"Because I do too."

Each gripped the phone tightly, not speaking. The truth filled the moment with a silent shout that penetrated the familiar roar of misunderstanding between them.

"What are we going to do, Hunter?"

Her voice was such a small whisper that he barely

could hear her. The quiet admission filled him with joy, and rainbows wrapped around his heart.

"We're going to fill those empty spaces with love, Mattie."

His hand clenched on the phone as he waited for her reply. Again the silence lengthened. Finally, he heard a soft click. Mattie wasn't ready to face the truth. He held the dead receiver to his ear until the electronic buzzing forced him to hang up.

He walked back to the window and looked across the hedge. Mattie's light went out. He smiled.

"The dark won't make the truth go away. You're going to be mine, Mattie Houston."

Seven

After the teddy-bear picnic, rehearsals became a cat-and-mouse game for Hunter and Mattie. They took turns being the cat, each bold in pursuit. Sometimes Mattie, dressed in clothes that would have vamped old Ebenezer Scrooge, would pop into Hunter's dressing room, drape herself on the edge of his dressing table, and play the coquette.

Hunter didn't care what her motives were; he was always delighted and amused.

"Hunter," she said on one of those occasions, "if I were a brazen woman, I'd kidnap you and take you far, far away."

"Why, Mattie?"

"I'd use you for my amusement."

"Are we talking fun and games?"

"No. Puppet shows. I especially adore your bear scenes."

"I'm willing to do a bare scene with you any time. Your place or mine?"

"It's no challenge if you're willing. The chase is more fun than the catch."

"If you think that, Mattie, then it's been too long since you've seen my catch."

The cat had hastened from the mouse's dressing room.

Then there were the times when Hunter did the stalking. He would stop in the middle of a puppet show, pull Mattie onto the stage, and catch her up in the magical, fanciful world of puppeteering.

Or he would slip up behind her during a rehearsal break, turn her around, and kiss her passionately. Then he'd release her and say, "Just getting my day's quota of loving."

The rest of the benefit cast became accustomed to their scandalous antics. Some of them were amused, others were tolerant, and still others made bets about who would do the chasing at the next rehearsal.

Mattie kept telling herself that she believed in Hunter's treachery, but each time she saw him, she believed more and more in his integrity. He was always totally honest with her. He made public declarations of his intent. He never pretended to be anything except the fun-loving, carefree rake that he was. And in spite of his tarnished reputation, she learned to trust him. She knew to expect the unexpected from him, though in serious matters such as the benefit, he was dedicated, enthusiastic, and hard-working. In spite of the game he played with her, he put together a professional-quality puppet show.

There was also the matter of his dream. She knew what it was like to dream. She also knew that too few people have the courage to pursue their dreams. Both she and Hunter had worked hard to make their career dreams come true. She admired him for that.

Still, she denied she was falling in love again. She told herself that her plan was working, that she could go back to Paris after the benefit, all her old scores settled, Hunter and the past finally put to rest.

Hunter knew better. Day by day he could sense the change in Mattie. He gauged her response to his kisses; he watched a blossoming of trust; he sensed the beginnings of forgiveness. Their time was coming. Soon.

Never one to sit back and wait, Hunter boldly carried out his campaign to win her. Every move he made was calculated. He knew when to be passionate and when to be tender. He knew when to be excessive and when to be steadfast. Mattie was the unfinished part of his dream, and nothing could stop him from fulfilling that dream.

Two days before the benefit concert, Hunter called Jackson, Mississippi.

"Hello." The voice at the other end of the line was lilting, cheerful, and every bit as beautiful as the woman it belonged to.

"Jessie, this is your favorite toy maker."

"Hunter! You sound wonderful! What are you doing? When are you coming to see us?"

He grinned at his childhood friend's excited chatter. "Us? Does that mean you're still married to that psychology professor?"

"Absolutely. You want to hear a secret, Hunter?"

"We've always shared secrets, Jessie."

"Blake's still magic."

Hunter's laughter was pure joy. If love could triumph for those two, he decided, it could certainly be as kind to him and Mattie. "How are the children?"

"Perfect angels. Baby Jess said her first word yesterday. Dada. The way Blake acted, you'd have thought she'd quoted the Gettysburg Address. Your namesake is more like you every day. A little friend of his at nursery school called himself a daredevil, and Chad declared that he was the 'mos' devil.' We'd love to see you, Hunter."

"You will. Pack a bag, Jessie. I want you and Blake to fly out to Dallas. There's somebody I want you to meet."

"Is it a woman? Has the most eligible bachelor in all of Dallas finally been caught?"

"It's a woman. Mattie Houston."

"The jazz pianist?"

"The same."

"Hunter! You've been holding out on me."

"I'm going to marry her, Jessie. I gave my blessing to you and Blake. Now I want yours. Mattie and I are in a benefit concert Friday night. Can you come?"

"We'll be on a plane tomorrow."

Mattie heard the music even before she opened her dressing-room door. There was no mistaking the sound. She knew she would find music boxes in the room. With her arms full of costumes and makeup, she nudged the door open with her hip and backed straight into Hunter.

He pulled her close. "If you keep this up, the concert will have to go on without its star."

She laughed. Nothing could daunt her tonight. She felt as if champagne were bubbling through her veins. Performances always did that to her. "If you don't let go, the star will have to perform in blue jeans. You're squashing my bugle beads."

He gave her one last squeeze, then let go. "Is that what they're called now?"

"You're crazy." She turned to hang up her clothes, and found herself surrounded by gardenias. They were everywhere—in baskets hanging from the ceiling, in vases on the dressing table, in cellophane wrappers on the floor. And among the gardenias, the carrousel music boxes spun round and round, tinkling their magic tunes.

The smile started in her heart and spread to her lips. She lifted her eyes to Hunter's face. "You did this."

"Yes."

"For old time's sake, Hunter?"

"No." He cupped her face. "For love's sake, Mattie. I love you."

He kissed her swiftly. It was over before she had time to gather her scattered wits.

"Break a leg, Mattie," he said. Then he was gone.

She stared at the closed door without really seeing it. Hunter filled her vision, arrogant, bold, witty, charming, and impossibly handsome in his tuxedo. His words echoed in her mind. "I love you, I love you, I love you."

She sank down on her knees and buried her face in a bouquet of gardenias. "It can't be true," she whispered. "It wasn't supposed to happen this way." The sweet perfume of the flowers filled her senses, and Hunter filled her heart. All of her carefully laid plans came crashing down, and she knew she'd been caught in the web of her own deceit. She'd flirted with him, thrown herself at him, until she finally got what she wanted. He'd fallen in love.

She lifted her head, fighting back the tears. What a fine scheme it had been, she thought. She'd have her revenge by breaking his heart. But she hadn't figured on her own emotions. She hadn't allowed for the irresistible pull of first love. And now not one heart would be broken, but two. The first time around she'd given her love to a reckless young dreamer, and the second time around she'd given it to a faithless womanizer.

Life was full of small ironies.

The tap on her door brought her out of her reverie. "Twenty minutes to curtain, Mattie," Jo Ann called.

With the self-control befitting her position as queen of jazz, Mattie put her problems aside and readied herself for the concert. She swept her glorious hair into an elegant French twist, made up her face with expert swiftness, and zipped into a tight-fitting, champagne-colored beaded evening gown.

She sparkled when she walked onstage. Even before she hit the first note, the audience was enthralled. As the glorious sounds of Mattie's jazz filled the auditorium, not a single person knew the struggle that was going on in her heart.

After the concert, Mattie signed autographs until Jo Ann rescued her.

"You were brilliant, Mattie." Jo Ann deftly cut a path through the crush of people. "But we have one more show to go. I don't want you exhausted before tomorrow's matinee."

They finally escaped the crowd and entered the dimly lit hallway backstage. Mattie stopped outside her dressing room door.

"Don't worry, Jo Ann," she said. "I'll be in fine form tomorrow."

Jo Ann nodded and hurried off.

A deep voice spoke from the shadows. "You always are in fine form, Mattie. I'm especially fond of your form in that dress."

Hunter was leaning against the doorway to his dressing room. As he walked toward her Mattie thought she'd never seen a man wear a tuxedo with such flamboyance and style. She was so mesmerized by him that she didn't notice the man and woman with him.

She covered her attraction by resorting to game-playing. "You're not so bad yourself. You look good enough to eat, as a matter of fact." She put her hand on the doorknob and smiled at him over her shoulder. "And I plan to."

"Promises, promises, Mattie."

"Have we come at a bad time, Hunter?" The voice was beautiful, musical, and definitely feminine.

Mattie whirled around. The woman standing beside Hunter had to be a model, she thought. Those cheek-bones and that black silk hair made her eyes look like sparkling green gems. A savage burst of jealousy ripped through Mattie. Damn Hunter's women. Why did he have to flaunt them in her face? Especially after that recent declaration of love. He was as insincere as a cat in a bird sanctuary. And just as dangerous.

She opened her mouth to vent her rage. Fortunately, a man with golden hair stepped out of the shadows and put his arms around the all-too-gorgeous woman.

"My wife and I loved your music, Miss Houston," the blond man said. "Hunter had told us about you, of course, and we've heard some of your recordings. But nothing had prepared us for your performance. You were electrifying."

Mattie barely heard a word he said after "wife." She would be forever grateful to him for speaking. Otherwise she might have committed murder right there on the spot.

She said, "Thank you." Or at least she thought she did. Hunter's grin was so wide and her legs were so weak with relief that she wasn't sure what she said.

"Mattie," Hunter said, "I want you to meet my dear friend, Jessie Wentworth, and her husband, Dr. Blake Montgomery."

Smiling, the stunning Jessie leaned toward Mattie. "Hunter grouched for a year because I kept my maiden name, but I've finally educated him in the ways of modern marriage. Fortunately, my husband wasn't so hard to convince. He knew from the beginning he was marrying a willful woman."

Mattie felt an immediate kinship with the woman she'd so recently wanted to murder. She glanced from Jessie to Blake Montgomery. Judging from the expression on his face, Mattie guessed he would have approved of anything his wife wanted.

"I'm delighted to meet both of you," she said. "Won't you come into my dressing room? It's a bit crowded, but it's better than standing in this dark hall."

"You don't know what you're asking, Mattie," Hunter said. "If Jessie ever gets you cornered in there, she'll spend three hours talking about her children."

Jessie laughed. "I've heard you wax eloquent on the subject, Hunter. Especially about your namesake."

"Blake Chadwick Montgomery. Now, there's a kid who's worth talking about." He grinned. "Remind me to tell you about him sometime, Mattie. He has the finest pitching arm east of the Mississippi. Besides that, he has my brilliance and my good looks. He even has my charm."

"And your modesty," Blake added. "Don't mind these two, Miss Houston. When they get together, they're irrepressible."

"Call me Mattie." She liked these people immensely. She liked their friendliness and their warmth, and she admired the obvious love they had for each other. But she liked them most for the way Hunter was with them, smiling and relaxed and perfectly content to talk about children. No, not just content, she corrected herself. Eager. Proud. That streak of domesticity surprised her, especially in view of his playboy's reputation. The last ten years he certainly hadn't behaved like a man interested in having a family. There had even been a scandal, a paternity suit. She'd always wondered whether the child was his.

Jessie linked her arm through Mattie's. "I'll go in and help you change. Hunter has planned a late dinner for all of us, and if we don't hurry I'll soon be eating the hall carpet. Being pregnant does that to me."

Hunter let out a whoop and scooped Jessie into his arms. "You're pregnant? Why didn't you two tell me?" He whirled Jessie before setting her back on her feet; then he clapped Blake on the back. "I envy you, old man."

Jessie patted Hunter's cheek. "Your time will come, friend," she said softly. Then she whisked Mattie into the dressing room.

Dinner was a lovely affair. Dallas was spread out below them, neon billboards flashing, street lights stretching for miles, gaudy and bright and beckoning, pulsing with a kind of raw excitement that only Texas can generate. Inside the restaurant, the foursome discovered how much they had in common. They laughed at Hunter's wit and argued good-naturedly about Blake's philosophy. They talked of music and art and toys and happiness. They discussed merchandising and politics and travel.

And all the while, Hunter and Mattie watched their two companions. Mattie saw the tender glances Blake gave his wife, and she felt envy. Hunter watched the way Jessie's hand kept stealing across the table to nestle in Blake's, and he felt deprivation. Mattie noticed how Blake's eyes lit up every time he looked at Jessie, and she longed to feel that loved. Hunter saw that Jessie glowed with contentment, and he was determined to put that same glow on the face of his Mattie.

After they had gone their separate ways—Mattie to her house, Hunter and his guests to his—the feeling persisted within Mattie that something precious was missing from her life.

She tiptoed into Papa's bedroom and gazed at the sleeping man. He looked so fragile in his sleep, his hair beginning to thin and his hands networked with delicate blue veins. He was all she had, she thought. And he was so old. She suddenly had a vision of her future, a vista of empty years stretching out before her, endless and lonely, with nothing but her music to stand between her and a sometimes-cruel world.

Bitterness rose in her. "Why did you do this to us, Hunter?"

She didn't realize she'd spoken aloud, until Papa stirred.

"Mattie? Is that you, honey?"

She sat on the edge of the bed and took his hand. "It's me, Papa. I didn't mean to wake you."

He sat up and propped himself against the headboard. Awake, he was once more the vital grandfather Mattie adored.

"Didn't mean to fall asleep. How was the concert?"

"It was marvelous. You're going to enjoy the matinee."

"I know I will. Are you going to play my favorite song, 'Our Love Is Here to Stay'?"

"Yes. Why do you love that song so much, Papa?"

"It expresses what your grandmother and I had. I wish you could have known her. My Mattie was something special. You're a lot like her, you know. Independent and spicy and beautiful. She was the most beautiful woman in the world. And I still miss her."

"I wish I could have known her, too, Papa. I wish I could have seen the two of you together. Daddy and Mother never expressed their love openly. I sometimes wonder if they even loved each other."

"William worshiped your mother. You too. You were the child of that love, and don't you forget it, Mattie."

"And my mother . . ." She left the sentence hanging. She felt guilty for probing. Her mother had been a special kind of woman, intense and high-strung and totally dedicated to her profession. But she had also been gay and lively and charming. Especially charming. Love welled up in her as she remembered her mother's charisma. Beside that glamorous appeal, Victoria's casual flirtations seemed insignificant, harmless manifestations of her exuberant spirit. Her aversion to loving touches, small hugs, and little pats on the cheek paled to nothingness. Mattie was lucky to have had such a wonderful mother, she assured herself.

"Your mother was . . . different, Mattie. People have various ways of showing how they feel." He squeezed her hand. "You're not like her. Not even remotely. Be yourself, Mattie."

"Thanks." She leaned over and kissed him. "Good night, Papa."

After she left, Phillip Houston lay in the darkness and cursed Victoria Houston.

Phillip Houston and Mickey Langston sat in the front row of the concert hall. Mattie's rendition of "Our Love Is Here to Stay" sent chills up the spines of the crowd.

"That's my granddaughter." Phillip's loud whisper carried three rows back.

Several people loudly shushed him.

"Wait'll you get a gander at my great-nephew." Uncle Mickey's whisper was equally as indiscreet.

More people hissed at him to be quiet.

"He's fine, all right," Phillip answered. "He's nearly good enough for my Mattie." His proud whisper rose another decibel.

Again, he was impatiently shushed.

"Damn bunch of sourpusses," Uncle Mickey declared.

"They obviously don't know who we are," Phillip Houston said.

After the concert was over, everybody knew who they were. They proclaimed it loud and long, to anyone who would listen. By the time Mattie and Hunter had made their way back to the front of the hall, the lively gentlemen were signing autographs.

"They're having so much fun, I almost hate to interrupt them," Hunter said. "Maybe we should sneak into our dressing rooms and let them have their moment of glory."

"Don't you dare, Hunter Chadwick. This is Papa's big moment. Watch." She strolled through the crowd until she was standing directly in front of Phillip; then she gave him a huge bear hug. "Papa! I'm so glad you came."

Phillip beamed at the crowd. "See. I *told* you she's my granddaughter."

Hunter joined them while the crowd laughed and vied for a place near the great jazz pianist. Some of them came close enough to touch her, others stood back and gazed in open-mouthed awe, and still others tried to satisfy their curiosity with questions.

"How long will you be in Dallas, Miss Houston? I've heard you're moving here."

"I'm going home to Paris day after tomorrow," Mattie said. The thought made her sad.

"Are you really engaged to that Russian prince?"

"Not yet," she said. She supposed a little white lie wouldn't hurt.

"Do you dye your hair?"

"No." She laughed at that one.

"I've heard you're in love with a Texan. Is that true?"

Her eyes were irresistibly drawn to Hunter's. "I don't have time for love," she said.

The crowd gradually dispersed. Mattie said good-bye to Papa and Uncle Mickey, then escaped to her dressing room. She leaned against the door, thankful to be away from the curious crowd and even more thankful to be away from Hunter's probing eyes.

Slowly she took the pins from her hair, then raked her fingers through the tumbled mass. She felt drained of energy, sapped of strength. It was just the usual letdown after a performance, she told herself. Certainly one man with sexy black eyes and a sometime-teddy-bear personality couldn't be the cause. She wondered if she'd made a mistake after dinner last night, agreeing to join Hunter at his lakeshore condominium for a little rest and relaxation after the performance today. How could an afternoon and evening with Hunter be restful and relaxing?

Someone tapped on her door just as she was reaching for the zipper on her dress.

"Come in," she called.

"I'll help you with that." Hunter was through the door and already unzipping her beaded gown before she could protest. "I think I'll take this as a permanent job."

He slowly slid the zipper down, running his hands along her bare back, making an erotic experience of the simple task. Mattie studied their reflections in the dressing-table mirror. They looked like any ordinary romantic couple, young, attractive, almost made for each other. It was a pity she couldn't believe the mirror, but it showed only the facade.

Hunter's lips nuzzled her neck as he slid the dress down her shoulders. She caught it before her breasts were exposed.

"Thanks, Hunter. I can take it from here."

He ignored her. "As I said, this is going to be a permanent job. I plan to make your bugle beads my personal business." His eyes devoured her as he brushed her hands aside and lowered the gown to her waist. "And I don't plan to share them with anybody. Especially not that damn Russian prince."

"That Russian-prince story was blown out of proportion by the newspapers." Somehow it seemed necessary to set the record straight. At least about that particular man. "We were never more than good friends."

Hunter gripped her shoulders. "Is that true, Mattie? It's important to me."

"It's true."

They stood silently, their eyes locked, watching and waiting for some sign, a signal that would have bridged the gap between them. In that moment of truth they might have crossed the chasm of misunderstanding, but Hunter made a fatal mistake: He revealed his private hell.

"One down and at least fifteen to go," he said.

His words were the red flag, and Mattie became the bull. Her head snapped back.

"How dare you!" She jerked herself free. Her hands shook as she pulled her gown over her bare breasts. "You're a fine one to talk about numbers. You've been in and out of every bed in Dallas. How dare you keep count of my lovers!"

"Mattie, I'm sorry." He moved toward her.

"Stop right there."

He kept coming. One more step and she was back in his arms. He held her so tightly, she could barely breathe.

"I admit to being a hypocrite. I admit to having double standards. But is that so wrong? A part of me still wants you to be the sweet innocent I fell in love with." He pulled her head down onto his shoulder and buried his face in her hair. "I love you, Mattie, just the way you are. I want you. No matter what."

Mattie fought against her feelings of tenderness. She denied her feelings of love. With great determination she held on to her rage. And out of that rage came the courage finally to settle her old score.

She lifted her head and looked up at him. "So you want me in spite of my fifteen lovers, do you? How would you like to be number sixteen?"

Gazing into her ice-green eyes, Hunter cursed himself. He'd have given anything in the world to take back his words, but it was no use. They'd already been said. The wedge had been driven between them once more. The trust that had been blossoming between them was crushed under the harsh blow of reality. Once more he was forced to take Mattie on her terms.

"You're on," he said grimly. "But be damned sure you mean it, because this time there won't be any back trouble to bail you out. Be ready to leave in fifteen minutes."

He stalked out, slamming the door behind him.

"I mean it, Hunter," she said to the closed door. "You'll rue the day you ever laid eyes on Mattie Houston."

She jerked off her beaded gown and quickly dressed in peach-colored linen slacks and a matching silk blouse. She crammed her gown and makeup into her bag and left. Her heels tapped an angry staccato as she marched down the hall to Hunter's dressing room. Without knocking, she shoved open the door.

"How does ten minutes suit you, Hunter?"

He was wearing nothing except his tuxedo pants. "Fine, Mattie. Have a seat. The suspenders and cummerbund take longer than your dress." He unzipped his pants and stepped out of them.

She pretended not to be impressed by him in his jockey shorts, but her eyes kept straying. And damn the luck, she thought, he would have to notice.

"See anything you like, Mattie?"

She licked her lips. He noticed that too.

"I never did trust a man who wore jockey shorts," she said.

"It doesn't matter. Trust seems to be in short supply between us."

"We have lust. That will suffice."

"For the time being."

She decided to let that remark pass.

He finished dressing and took her arm. "Let's go."

He marched her resolutely down the hall and into the parking lot. There he threw their bags into the trunk of his car, then pulled recklessly out onto the street. Mattie stared straight ahead, staunchly maintaining her attitude of not caring. Her chest was tight, and she felt as if there were no air left in the world to breathe.

The late-afternoon sun burned down on Dallas, scorching the asphalt streets until the heat seemed to rise up and smother the travelers. Even the air conditioning in the car couldn't dispel the suffocating sensation.

Mattie longed for Paris. She longed for the Champs Elysees and the Arc de Triomphe. She longed for the fountains and flowers and bustle of busy people who didn't care whether she'd had fifteen lovers or none.

Slanting her eyes toward Hunter, she stole a look at him. He might have been one of the stone statues in the Place de la Concorde, remote and cold. His expression froze her heart, and she shivered.

"Cold, Mattie? I'll turn on the heat."

She was surprised he'd noticed. "Save the heat for the bedroom."

His jaw tightened. Handling the car as if it were an angry stallion, he whipped down an exit ramp. Mattie saw that they were headed east, toward Ray Hubbard Lake and Hunter's condominium, just as they'd planned the night before.

She wanted to yell, "Stop the car and let me out." She wanted to scream, "I take it all back." But it was too late. The car ate up the miles as Hunter ignored speed limits in his single-minded determination to reach his destination. In grim silence they arrived at his condominium on the lake.

"This is it," he said. "If you can restrain yourself that long, I'll unload the bags and we can get a bite to eat."

She clenched her fists. "Fine. Making you number sixteen is not at the top of my list of my favorite things to do."

Some small voice of sanity seemed to penetrate his consciousness.

"Then why are you doing it?" he asked.

She saw the change in him, noticed the softening of his face. It was almost as if he were offering her a way out. Almost, but not quite.

"It's been a long time since Paris," she said, "and I'm a woman with an appetite." She got out of the car and slammed the door. Looking at him across the top of the Maserati, she added, "Lead on, Hunter."

He stomped around to the back of the car and took out the luggage. He wanted to tell her to stop it, but couldn't. All this was his fault anyway. He was the one who had ruined a perfectly good weekend by bringing up the subject of her lovers. He had planned this weekend so carefully. He had meant it to be a time of love and healing. One careless remark had changed it into another of their pitched battles.

Neither of them noticed the elegance of his apartment, all open spaces and gleaming glass and chrome tables and plush modern furniture; nor did they notice the way the sun seemed to beam a benediction through the enormous skylight and the bank of windows facing the lake. They were too busy going through their separate hells.

Hunter dumped the bags in one of the bedrooms, then went to the kitchen. Mattie sat stiffly on the sofa while he threw together peanut butter and jelly sandwiches. When he was finished he leaned across the bar to call her. The sight of her sitting there, looking so stiff and remote and somehow vulnerable, ripped at his gut. He wanted to call the whole thing off and start over, but it was too late.

"Food's ready, Mattie."

She walked toward him, moving as if she might break at every step. Holding her back very straight, she sat on the edge of her chair and bit into a sandwich. Hunter watched every move she made.

"Aren't you going to eat too?" she asked.

"No."

She was acutely aware that he wasn't going to make this easy for her. She thought of all the narrow escapes she'd had, all the windows she climbed out of, all the apartments she had fled in the middle of the night. This time, though, there would be no escape. Hunter was the kind of man who got exactly what he wanted.

The silence thundered around them.

"I hate peanut butter." The sound of her own voice was small comfort in the agony of defeat that surrounded her. At this point it didn't matter that she would sleep in Hunter's bed and then leave for Paris. It didn't matter that she might leave him with a broken heart again. It didn't matter that she might make him pay for the past. What mattered was the crushing defeat of coming so close to building something beautiful on the ashes of the past, only to have it torn away by a few angry words.

They were careless people after all, she and Hunter. Love was such a fragile thing, and they didn't know how to treat it with care. She had the frightening realization that she was reliving Victoria's life. Now she was the one seeking to find meaning through casual liaisons. Except that Hunter wasn't casual. He was so much a part of her that she felt as if she were lacerating herself.

She put her half-eaten sandwich on the plate. Now was not the time for regrets. Hunter was watching her with that look of pure sex in his eyes, and she had the rest of the day and tomorrow before she returned to Paris. She stood up.

"Which bedroom, Hunter?"

"This way." He took her elbow and led her down the hall.

In the bedroom she turned her back to him, stripped off her blouse, and threw it across a chair. She felt his eyes on her back. Turning around, she gave him a cold stare. He was leaning against the doorframe.

"Aren't you coming in?" she asked.

"You've done nothing to make me want to come in, Mattie. For a practiced hoyden, your style lacks finesse."

"Damn you, Hunter." She flew across the room and struck his chest with her fists. "Damn you for making me do this."

He caught her wrists. "I thought this was what you wanted."

She kicked his shin. "Let go of me."

He held her fast. "Are you trying to tell me you've changed your mind? Are you trying to say this is not the way you want us to be, cold and calculating and vengeful?"

"Dammit! Turn me loose." She felt her breath whoosh out as he scooped her into his arms and held her tightly against his chest. He kicked the door shut, then stalked across the room and dumped her unceremoniously onto the bed. Then she was crushed beneath his weight.

"I don't intend to let you go, Mattie. I've already told you that. We can have this any way you want it—your way or mine."

"And what is yours, Hunter? To get some helpless woman pregnant and deny the child?"

His eyes went as black as doom. "You know about the paternity suit." It was not a question.

"It was headline news."

"Trumped-up garbage always is." He shifted himself off her, rolling onto his side and pinning her down with his legs.

She struggled to rise.

"You're not going anywhere until you hear the truth, Mattie. I think it's high time there was truth between us."

"Save your breath, Hunter. You lied to me ten years ago. I have no reason to believe anything you say is the truth."

"We'll let the past go for now. It's the present I want to set straight. Let's level with each other about our reputations."

"My fifteen lovers, you mean?"

"Dammit! Forget that remark. I don't care if you've had fifteen lovers or fifteen hundred. I'm still going to marry you."

"I won't be another of your playthings, Hunter."

"Do you want to know how many lovers I've had in the last ten years, Mattie?"

She covered her ears and squinched her eyes shut. "No!"

"You're going to hear the truth whether you want to or not." He peeled her hands away from her ears. "I've had two. In all the years you've been gone, I've found solace with only two women. And they were damned poor substitutes for you."

In spite of herself, she was interested. "I saw pictures in the society pages, Hunter. Do you deny all those others?"

"Yes. They were merely social climbers I kept happy with a kiss on the lips and a pat on the butt."

"And what about the child, Hunter? Do you also deny your own child?"

"I have no child. When Andrea brought the paternity suit against me, I almost wished it were mine. But it wasn't true. We'd been lovers, all right. For six months. But Dad's investigators were thorough. They discovered that Andrea hadn't been faithful. She had a little something going on the side. A night-club manager. He'd moved in the month I was away on business. The time of conception wasn't right for me to have been the father. Also, there have been advances made in methods of testing for paternity. The blood tests proved beyond a doubt that he was the father. Andrea and Wayne both knew that. They saw opportunity in the form of the Chadwick bank account."

Hunter caught her face between his hands. "Open your eyes and look at me, Mattie."

She opened one eye, then shut it. "I don't care, Hunter."

"Yes, you do." His hands became gentle as he caressed her face. "Your skin is clammy, Mattie. There's no need to be afraid."

"I'm not afraid."

"I think you are. Why?"

Her eyes flew open. "Because I don't want you to be fine and good and noble. I want you to be a callous rake so I can hate you."

"You don't hate me, do you, Mattie?"

"No," she whispered. Her eyes were bright with unshed tears. "Heaven help me, Hunter, I've fallen in love with you again."

The sunshine of his smile lit up the room.

"That's all I need to know, Mattie. That you love me."

She bit her lip as indecision ripped at her. "I'm not ready for this, Hunter. In spite of what you've said, I can't let go of my old feelings so easily."

"I won't hurt you. I'll never hurt you again." His expression was unbearably tender as he looked down at her. He smoothed her hair back from her forehead, stroked her cheeks, traced her lips. "There will be no more games between us." He sat up, pulling her with him. "Put on your blouse, Mattie."

"Why?"

"I'm taking you out for a proper dinner. Candlelight and violins and waiters who fall in the soup trying to be helpful. And while we're there you can talk of anything you please. Or not talk at all, if that pleases you."

"And afterward?"

"We'll come back here and start all over again. Only this time, there'll be nothing between us except the truth."

Eight

"Only two, Hunter?" Mattie asked. She looked up from her soup and wondered how she could ever have denied her feelings for this tender teddy-bear man.

"Only two what?"

"You know what I'm talking about."

"Candlelight becomes you, Mattie."

"Candlelight makes you look yummy gorgeous, Hunter, but you still didn't answer my question."

He smiled at her over the rim of his wineglass. "I think I'll start carrying candles in my pockets. Flattery will get you everywhere, princess."

"Hunter!"

He laughed, loving her impatience, loving her interest in him. "Yes. Only two."

"I'm jealous of them both. I hope they had baggy butts and bad breath and warts."

"Only warts."

She toyed with her soup, then finally gave up all pretense of eating. A waiter whisked it away when the spoon was barely out of her hand. She laughed.

"You were right about these waiters, Hunter. That one did almost fall into my soup."

"You know what I've missed most about you, Mattie?"

"My elegant body?"

"Your laughter." He reached across the table and stroked her long fingers. "Nobody in the world laughs like you, full-throated and uninhibited. I used to hear it in my dreams. I'd get out of bed and walk to the window to see if you were standing in Phillip's courtyard. Sometimes I'd imagine I heard it on the street, and I'd follow the sound." He grinned. "I've chased more strange women down the street that way. Caught a few of them, too. Got me into a heap of trouble. One of them even hit me with her purse and called me a pervert."

Mattie loved it. She loved his humor, his confessions, his sincerity, his honesty. She loved knowing that he, too, had been holding onto a dream. She loved knowing that his lovers had been substitutes, attempts to blot out their summer romance. And she knew it was time for her own confession.

"You know what I've missed most about you, Hunter?"

"My prodigious part?"

They both burst into laughter. It was an old joke between them. Once they'd whiled away a sunny afternoon on the beach thinking of new and bizarre ways to describe each other. Two of their favorites had been her doorway to paradise and his prodigious part. They laughed so hard, they never even noticed the waiter bringing their salad.

"No," she finally said. "Your eyes. Everything you're thinking shows in those black eyes. I used to search other dark eyes, hoping I'd see that gleam of amber yours always had when you were feeling happy or passionate." She smiled. "I was hoping to find that look you have right now."

"Did you, Mattie?"

She ignored the question. "And your voice, Hunter. Sometimes when you speak I feel as if I've been caressed by velvet. In ten years, I could never forget that voice."

Hope soared in him. He held her hand tightly, not

speaking, afraid of breaking the fragile trust he could sense growing between them. With the strength of his hand, he communicated his need and his love.

"I tried so hard to hate you," she continued. "And at first I did. But after all the rage had subsided, I knew that you were still a part of me. What we had together— the discovery of first love—could never be forgotten. And so I tried to replace you. I came close with the Russian prince."

She squeezed his hand and drew a deep breath. There was no turning back now. Whatever happened, she was committed to telling the truth. At least a part of it. She still couldn't bring herself to discuss what had happened ten years ago. It was best forgotten. He'd been young, and her mother . . . No, she decided. She just wouldn't think about it. The revenge she'd thought she wanted had somehow been changed to forgiveness. And it felt good. It felt so good that she didn't want to disturb it.

"Hunter?"

"What is it, Mattie?"

"Do you truly love me?"

"I love you more than I ever thought possible. All the things you are have wrapped around my heart and bound me forever. I loved you when you were eighteen, I love you now, and I'll love you when you're ninety-five." He lifted her hand to his lips. "And I don't ever intend to let you go."

The touch of his lips branded her, and she was his.

"There was never anyone except you," she said quietly.

Hunter felt the shock of her words all the way down to his toes. Joy ignited his soul. His hand tightened on hers.

"Mattie?"

"Lord knows I tried. I wanted to fall in love again. And when that didn't work, I even tried to be casual and sophisticated and nonchalant about the whole thing." She laughed. "My reputation far exceeds my exploits. I've climbed out more windows and shinned down more trees than a cat burglar." Her green eyes sparkled at him over the untouched salad. "I love you, Hunter. I don't think I ever stopped."

"Are you hungry, Mattie?"

"Only for you."

He pulled her up with one hand and reached into his pocket with the other. He tossed a hundred-dollar bill on the table, then hastened her through the restaurant. He didn't even notice their waiter running along behind them, sputtering and red-faced and astonished.

The waiter caught up with them in the foyer. If it hadn't been such a high-class establishment, he probably would have shouted. But he had been well trained in circumspect behavior. "Sir," he said.

Hunter turned. "The money's on the table. Eat the lobster yourself. Call your girl and share it with her. This is a celebration. Compliments of Hunter Chadwick."

Hunter didn't let go of Mattie's hand even when they got into the car. He held on while he turned the key and still held on as he backed out of the parking space.

"Handy talent to have," he said, smiling at her. "Driving with one hand." They whizzed through the night, wrapped in a cocoon of love.

"Don't ever let go, Hunter," she said. The firm touch of his hand conveyed such strength, such purpose, such promise, that she wanted to feel it always, through her times of sunshine and through her times of darkness.

"I won't, Mattie."

"Even if I forget how much I love you, promise you won't ever let me go."

"I promise." He lifted her hand to his lips. "I don't intend to be away from you long enough for you to forget."

"Remember how it was the first time we loved?"

"Yes. You were scared."

"I was not. You were the one who had goose bumps."

"That's because of what your hands were doing to my prodigious part."

She laughed. "As I recall, you did a few wonderful things yourself."

"I plan to do even better this time around."

"If it's any better, Hunter, you can just cover my body with gardenias and tell everybody I've gone on to paradise."

"I plan to cover your body with more than gardenias." He guided her hand down his flat stomach and into his lap.

She squeezed. The car swerved perilously near a ditch. Still using only one hand on the wheel, Hunter got them back on the road.

"Watch it, Mattie. That thing's liable to explode."

"I hope so."

"Did anybody ever tell you that you're a wicked woman?"

The tires squealed as he turned into his driveway.

"Hurry and park the car," she said. "I plan to show you just how wicked I can be."

They ran together across the moonlit yard and into his dark apartment. He stopped inside the door and pulled her into his arms.

"Do you hear something, Mattie?"

She snuggled her head into the wonderful indention just over his heart. And she knew contentment. "What?"

"I hear the bed. It's calling our names."

Her arms circled his neck as she looked up at him. "I've missed you, sweet teddy-bear man."

"And I've missed you, my beautiful summer-jazz woman."

Their kiss was like coming home. It was summer sunshine and soft sea breezes and first love rediscovered. It was jazz and laughter and dreams remembered. And it was more, much, much more. It was love affirmed and promises renewed. It was trust and respect and forgiveness.

Hunter devoured her lips, trying to make up for ten years in one heady moment. His lips moved down her throat, nudged aside her blouse. His tongue wet the fragrant valley between her breasts.

"Do you know how long I've waited for this?" he asked. "How often I've dreamed of this?" He pulled her so close, she felt as if their hearts meshed. "When I think of those wasted years!"

She tangled her hands in his hair, urging his head down so that it was buried between her breasts. "Forget the empty years. Love me, Hunter."

He lifted her and carried her down the hallway to his bedroom. Even in the dark she could see the gleam in his eyes, that amber gleam that had followed her across an ocean and through a span of lonely years. She wanted to laugh and to cry. But most of all she wanted to be loved by this man.

He kicked the door shut behind them. For a moment he was still, holding her against his thundering heart.

"Forgive me, Mattie, for waiting so long."

He didn't need to say more. That simple statement encompassed all the stubbornness and false pride and guilt and misunderstanding that had separated them.

"I forgive you, Hunter."

She forgave him more than the waiting. She forgave the past, freeing herself to love again.

He let her slide down his body until her feet touched the floor. He still held her so close that his heartbeat felt like her own. They clung to each other in the moonlight, their eyes saying a thousand things.

Suddenly he moved. His hands unbuttoned and unzipped and unhooked. Their clothes fell in a tangled heap at their feet. He carried her to the bed and lowered her into the patch of moonlight that was spilling across the covers.

"You're a dream come true," he said.

She lifted her arms to him. "Lie with me. I'm real."

He knelt beside her, discovering her with his hands. His fingertips glided across her cheekbones, traced her lips, outlined her chin. "I remember your skin. Soft, so soft."

She pressed his hands to her face. "And I remember your hands, the gentleness, the strength. Your touch makes me feel safe, Hunter."

He lay down beside her, pulling her into his arms, smoothing her glorious fire-and-sunshine hair. He rocked her against his body, feeling the way they fit together, custom-made for each other, loving how her nipples peaked, diamond-hard and ready against his chest, reveling in her long legs wrapping around his, trim and silken and parted.

His hands were on her back, kneading, pressing, caressing. Her lips were on his throat, kissing, sucking, devouring. He arched away from her and took one of the taut nipples in his mouth.

"Oh, yes, Hunter. Like that." He suckled. She moaned. "Always, I remembered how that felt."

He couldn't get enough of her. The moon highlighted his dark hair and slanted across his square jaw as he feasted on her breasts, bringing them both to the point of explosion. "Mattie . . . my Mattie." His hungry mouth and tongue left her breasts and traced every silken inch of her body, tasting, nibbling, wetting, entering, thrusting.

"Do you remember this, Mattie?" His voice was slurred, drunken with love.

"Yes. But . . . never . . . this . . . good." She dug her fingernails into his back. Her head pressed into the pillows as sensations rocked her. He was her first love, her only love. It had been ten years and it had been only yesterday. His touch was as familiar and cherished as a favorite childhood toy. And yet it was new. Exciting. And almost unbearably erotic.

"Hunter!" Her plea echoed in the moon-bright, love-bright room.

His eyes gleamed amber as he lifted over her. He entered. She arched. He thrust. She moaned. They exploded. And all of Dallas was bright with their love.

"I've . . . waited . . . so long . . . for this." His words

were thick as he rolled onto his back, carrying her with him.

He plunged. She rode. He groaned. They ignited. And all of Texas caught fire.

The pattern of moonlight moved down the bed as Hunter and Mattie renewed their love. When it had settled around their feet, their cries of fulfillment shattered the stillness.

She lay slack across his chest, her hair covering his cheek, her legs tangled with his.

He kissed her damp forehead. "Delicious."

She caressed his face. "Remarkable."

"Stupendous."

"Yummy."

"Mind-boggling."

"Magic."

He laughed. "A Hunter Chadwick superspecial."

She reached down and pinched his butt. "Has anybody ever told you that you're the most arrogant man in Texas?"

"But you love it, don't you, Mattie?"

"Yes." She nuzzled his neck. "I don't think we can ever make up for all those lost years."

He held her close. "We have the rest of our lives, Mattie."

She raised herself on her elbows and grinned down at him. "I was thinking more in terms of tonight."

"You were, were you?"

"Yes."

"I think I can manage that." He moved his hips, and the magic started all over again. It lasted until the first rosy blush of dawn began to pink the sky, and then they slept.

When they woke up, it was raining. Fat droplets splatted against the windows and hammered on the roof. The sky, the lake, even the bedroom, had turned a gloomy gunmetal gray.

The gloom didn't daunt the lovers, though. Love was

their sunshine. Hunter snuggled Mattie, spoon fashion, against his body.

"How about a picnic on the beach?" he asked.

"In this rain? Are you crazy?"

"No. Just a little oversexed."

"How little?"

He guided her hand. "That little."

"That's not little. That's shocking."

"Then, Mattie, I suggest you do something about it before it gets out of hand."

And she did.

Much later Mattie was chin-deep in bubbles when Hunter banged on the bathroom door.

"Quick. Get your swimsuit. We're going to the beach."

"Is the sun shining?"

He opened the door and grinned at her. "Who needs sunshine when I'm around? Hurry, Mattie, or I'll be forced to get into the tub and burst a few of those bubbles."

She scooped up a handful of bubbles and blew them at him. "You're invited."

"Good Lord, woman. I'm a mere man, not Superman."

"Chicken."

He plunged through the door, stripping as he walked. "Never let it be said that Hunter Chadwick backed down from a challenge."

Bubbles spilled over the edge of the tub as he climbed into the water. Mattie wrapped her soapy arms around him and began nibbling his neck.

"Hmmm. Yummy," she said.

He laughed. "The wonderful thing about women too long deprived is their insatiability."

Her head snapped back. "Why, you—"

He stopped her words with his mouth. By the time they finally got out of the tub, all the bubbles had disappeared and the water had turned cold.

Hunter wrapped them in huge towels and carried Mattie back to the bedroom.

"Picnic-on-the-beach time, Mattie. Get into your swimsuit."

She glanced toward the window. "It's still raining, Hunter."

He set her on her feet and swatted her bottom. "No, it's not. The sun's shining, the waves are lapping against the shore, and the coconut trees are swaying."

"Coconut trees? In Dallas?" She put a hand on his brow. "Do you have a fever? I think lack of sleep has affected your brain."

"It affected parts of me, but not my brain. Put on your swimsuit." He unknotted her towel and dropped it to the floor. The amber light gleamed in his eyes as he raked her from head to toe. "On the other hand, we could forget about the coconuts." He dropped his towel.

"Look who was just talking about deprivation. Put on your swimsuit." She crossed the room and stepped into a swimsuit that was so sexy, it could have started a revolution. "Lead me to the coconut trees, Hunter."

He didn't move.

"Hunter?"

He lifted his gaze to her face. "If ten years can make you that much more beautiful, you'll be too much for a man to bear by the time you're forty-eight."

She walked over to him and looked deep into his remarkable black eyes. "Have I told you today how much I love you?"

"I never get tired of hearing it."

"I love you, Hunter Chadwick."

"Don't ever forget that, Mattie."

"I promise."

He lowered his head and took her lips. The kiss was as light as summer rain and as tender as the first daffodils of spring. When it was over, he put on his swimsuit and led her to the den.

Cardboard trees with crepe paper branches bent under their burden of real coconuts, attached with wire.

A giant sunlamp gleamed through a yellow umbrella. A small, child's pail, filled with sand, stood on the floor beside two striped red-and-yellow towels. A wicker picnic hamper rested under the umbrella sun.

"The beach, princess."

"You did all this, Hunter?"

"Yes. Just for you."

"Why? We could have had a picnic in the kitchen."

"As I recall, some of our best conversations took place on the beach." He pulled her down onto the towels. "It's time to talk, Mattie."

"I'd rather just stay here forever, loving and laughing and forgetting. Especially forgetting."

"We have to face the truth. We've already partially bared our souls. Let's not stop now."

She picked up a handful of sand and let it drizzle through her fingers. "I've forgiven you for what happened. Isn't that enough?"

He wanted to explode. He wanted to bash his fist onto the floor and shout, "Nothing happened!" But if the last few days had taught him anything, they had taught him the damning effect of words spoken in haste. He reined in his impatience.

"A relationship must be built on trust," he said. "Complete trust." He took her hand out of the child's pail and wiped off the sand. "Look at me, Mattie." She lifted her eyes to his face. "Let's talk about what happened. Let's put the past to rest."

Her eyes widened. "I don't know why you'd want to talk about something that . . . treacherous." His hand tightened on hers, and a small muscle twitched in his clenched jaw. "Please, Hunter!" She leaned her face against his shoulder. "I love you, and I've put the past behind by forgetting it. It's not important anymore. Can't you let it go at that?"

He held her fiercely against his chest. "I'll take you, Mattie, any way I can get you."

They clung together, afraid to let go, afraid that breaking the contact would sever the fragile trust that bound them. The rain assaulted the windows and a deepening gloom penetrated the room, but Hunter and Mattie sat under their false sun and held on to their false hopes. They talked of her extending her stay in Dallas long enough for a wedding. They talked of going back to Paris together, a combined honeymoon and settling of her affairs. They talked of making Dallas their permanent home and keeping her Paris apartment. They discussed how they would juggle two careers and a family. They both wanted children, lots of them.

But the niggling doubts Hunter's questions had raised, stayed in the back of their minds. Mattie wondered if a part of her would always mistrust him because of what had happened ten years ago, and Hunter wondered how he could accept her terms. He didn't like the idea of being forgiven for something he hadn't done. What was worse, he didn't even know what the hell she had hated him for.

Their initial joyous exuberance was missing as they finished the weekend at his condominium. Their laughter was restrained, and their lovemaking had a desperate edge to it, as if they were trying to store away something precious that might be snatched from them.

By the time they started back to Dallas, Mattie knew she'd eventually have to face the truth and that Hunter was determined to find it.

Uncle Mickey had spiffed himself up just to walk through the hedge to Phillip's house. He didn't try to fool himself. Ever since his talk with Hunter, he'd been thinking about Janet Cleary, about all the love they'd had, about all the lonesome years without her. He'd finally decided that it might not be too late, after all. If he was still spry enough to climb in and out of a toy box, surely he was spry enough to climb in and out of Janet's bed.

The thought made him quicken his step. He punched

the bell, then straighened his tie. No need for Janet to see him looking rumpled.

The door swung open. "Let me take your umbrella," Janet said. Her manner was stiff, formal. "Mr. Houston's expecting you."

"He can wait. I want to talk to you."

"About what?" Only a small trembling of her lips betrayed Janet's turmoil.

"Us."

"That was over a long time ago."

Mickey took her hand and lifted it to his lips. "It was never over for me, Janet. I've been a fool to wait this long to tell you."

Janet patted her severe bun with her free hand. "Just look at me. I must be a fright, all starchy and dried-up and old." Her eyes were stricken. "I'm old, Mickey."

"You're beautiful." He touched her face. "And I still want you as much as I did twenty years ago. Have dinner with me tonight, Janet."

"I shouldn't."

"Why?"

"My life is ordered, Mickey. Dull, but pleasant. Having dinner with you won't change what I am—a wrinkled old woman who let life pass her by."

Mickey's eyes twinkled. "Don't you know I'm a wizard? I create kings and kingdoms. I make dragons that breathe fire and men that fly. Have dinner with me and I'll make you young again. I'll make both of us young again."

"Well . . ."

"Say yes. I'm getting older by the minute."

Janet Cleary laughed. It was a young laugh, gay and uninhibited, and surprising, coming from such a drawn, tired mouth. "Yes."

"Get ready to be fept off your sweet, woman. I'll pick you up at seven."

They were both laughing as she escorted him to Phillip's study.

"I hope that laughter means what I think it means," Phillip said to Mickey.

"It does. I'm taking Janet out."

"High time. Sit down. We have something serious to discuss. Damned serious."

"It must be, to call me away from my afternoon martoonie. And in this rain, to boot."

"Martini, hell." Phillip stood up and performed a series of karate kicks. "You'd do well to leave the martinis and work out with me. Did you see that form? That body control? That muscle tone?" He chuckled. "It might come in handy when you get Janet between the sheets."

Mickey laughed. "You're a horny old coot."

"That's right. Meddlesome, too." Phillip sat back down and propped his elbows on the arms of his chair. "Mattie called me from Hunter's condo. It seems that nephew of yours kidnapped her. She didn't sound too unhappy about it."

"Damned brilliant boy."

"He came to see me not long ago. Asked if I knew why Mattie returned his ring ten years ago."

"He asked me the same thing."

"It got me to thinking. Yesterday after the matinee I suddenly remembered an envelope Victoria had given me that summer. She told me it contained pictures that we should keep from William. She knew I was aware of her tawdry affairs. She also knew I'd do anything to spare my son the shame. So I entered into a conspiracy with that witch. Put the envelope into the safe without ever looking inside. I didn't want to know what it contained—until yesterday." He handed Mickey a large manila envelope. "Take a look at that."

Mickey pulled three black-and-white glossy photographs from the envelope. Angry red patches mottled his face as he looked at the pictures. The first one showed Victoria stepping into a hot tub—Hunter's hot tub—and a tall, dark-haired man embracing her from behind. In the next picture she was sitting in the tub, her hands pinned behind her on the tiled rim, and the man was kissing her. Not just a man, but Hunter. Even though the pictures were fuzzy and taken from a distance, there was no mistaking that profile. In the third picture, her torn swimsuit was in the foreground, and Hunter lay atop her in the tub. Again, his profile was plainly visible. Or was it Hunter's profile? Mickey wondered. He leaned down for a closer look. Something was not quite right. It was the hair. Even after a thorough brushing, Hunter's hair had never been that tame.

He tossed the pictures onto a marble-topped coffee table. "That's not Hunter."

"You're sure?"

"Damned right! Number one, the hair's not right. Number two, Hunter would never do anything as despicable as seducing the mother of the woman he loved."

"Looks more like rape to me."

Mickey half rose from his chair. "We've been friends all these years and you say that about my nephew!"

"Sit down, Mickey. I didn't say I thought it was your nephew. At first I did. I went into such a rage that I kicked a two-thousand-dollar Chinese porcelain vase down the stairs. Broke it all to hell and back."

"I never did like that vase."

"Neither did I." Phillip picked up the pictures and stuffed them back into the envelope. "Then I got to thinking." He tapped the envelope. "This is out of character for Hunter—but exactly the kind of scheme that vicious woman would devise. She had the soul of a rattlesnake."

"I always felt sorry for her. It was sad to see a woman who had everything and didn't know it."

"Don't waste your sympathy. She was a slut. I never knew why William shut his eyes to the truth." Phillip gazed off into space. "Mattie's like her father in that way."

"When the truth is too hard to live with, people create fantasies."

Phillip shot his friend an appreciative look. "What are we going to do about these damned pictures?"

Mickey didn't hesitate. "Show Hunter. Obviously Victoria used them to break up her daughter's romance. Though I can't for the life of me imagine why."

"I can. Mattie was competition. She had youth and beauty—two things Victoria was losing."

"Hunter has to know. Otherwise he'll spend the rest of his life paying for a crime he didn't commit."

"You're right. Take them." Phillip handed the envelope to Mickey. "I hope we're doing the right thing."

The pictures made Hunter sick with rage. "Damned slut!" He kicked a chair. It sailed across the room and smashed into the fireplace grate. "If she weren't dead already, I'd wring her neck."

Mickey watched silently as his nephew vented his anger.

"Ten years! Ten years wasted because of her." He swept his hand across his desk top, sending papers flying in every direction. "No wonder Mattie hated me."

Suddenly he slumped into a chair and buried his face in his hands. "Oh, God . . . Mattie! How can I tell her?"

"You have to, Hunter." Uncle Mickey was the voice of sanity in the midst of madness. "If you gloss it over, pretend it never happened, it'll fester between you and eventually destroy your love."

Hunter looked up. His face was haggard. "She says she's forgiven me."

"For what? You didn't do anything."

The blackness of despair was in Hunter's eyes as he pondered his dilemma. Mattie would be hurt again. She'd lived with the false knowledge of his guilt, and now she had to face the truth of her mother's guilt. No wonder she kept backing away from the past. Could he burn the pictures and forget about them? Could he and Mattie still have a good marriage? He knew the answer. No. His guilt was a lie, and a marriage based on a lie would never survive.

His hand clenched around the damning pictures as he stood up. "Pray that I can do this without losing Mattie."

Hunter didn't waste any time. He walked straight out of his house and through the hedge. A light was beaming down from the music room. He looked up. Mattie was silhouetted at the piano. He felt as if an iceberg were pressing against his heart. "Let our love be strong enough to survive this," he said as he strode across the courtyard. Nobody heard except the crickets.

Phillip answered the door. His sharp old eyes didn't miss the lines of tension around Hunter's mouth, the envelope in his hand. "I'm sorry about all this, son. Maybe it would be best if we just put the pictures back in the safe and pretended I never took them out."

"No. The truth has to be told. The air has to be cleared between us once and for all."

Phillip nodded. "She's upstairs . . . practicing. Be gentle."

"I will. I love her."

Hunter took the stairs two at a time. He heard her long before he reached the room. The music was bold and sultry and beautiful—like the woman who was playing it, he thought. He stood in the hallway for a moment, letting the music seep into his soul. Then he walked through the door and straight to Mattie.

"I could listen to your music forever," he said, placing his hands on her shoulders. "And I plan to."

"Hunter!" She swiveled around and hugged him. "I didn't hear you come in." She made room for him on the piano bench. "I didn't expect to see you again until tomorrow. ML day."

"What's ML?"

"Marriage license." She laughed, and Hunter thought it was a sound that rivaled her music. "Don't tell me you've changed your mind."

He caught her against his chest in a desperate embrace. "Never. I never intend to let you go, Mattie."

She rubbed her cheek against his shirt. "Hmmm. You smell wonderful. Like summer wind." She popped open his top button and nibbled. "I think I'll eat you."

Hunter wrestled with his control. He wanted to lower her to the floor and bury himself in her soft flesh in blissful forgetfulness. But the envelope in his hand was a vivid reminder of what he had to do.

"Phillip's downstairs," he said.

"We'll lock the door."

"Mattie."

Something in his voice made her look up. All the demons of hell seemed to be gazing out of his eyes. The taste of fear rose in her throat. She gripped his shoulders so hard, her fingernails bit into his flesh. Not now, her mind screamed. Not when everything's going so well. Please, God, don't let anything else happen to us.

Time was suspended as they looked into each other's eyes. The minutes dragged by in raging silence. Everything was magnified: the lines around Hunter's mouth. The beads of sweat on Mattie's upper lip. The pulse hammering in his throat. The whiteness of her knuckles.

She closed her eyes for an instant and drew in a long breath. She wouldn't let anything happen. Slowly she relaxed her grip. The toss of her head and the gay lilt of her voice camouflaged her fear.

"I'm not accustomed to being turned down. Don't tell me you're already tired of me."

"We have to talk." He stood up, lifting her with him, and moved toward the sofa.

For the first time Mattie noticed the envelope, Victoria's bold scrawl in red ink across the left-hand corner. She felt as if she were falling into a dark hole.

"No."

Her whisper ripped at Hunter's gut. Gently he pulled her down beside him.

"I've seen the pictures, Mattie."

"How?" Her fingernails bit into his arm.

"They were in Phillip's safe. All these years, he thought he was protecting your father by keeping them. It wasn't until after my visit a while ago that he looked to see what they were."

She pounded his chest with her fists. "You had no right. No right!"

He caught her wrists. "I'm not the man in the pictures, Mattie."

A sob caught in her throat. "Damn you, Hunter. I had forgiven you."

He pulled her, stiff and unyielding, into his arms. "I wish there were an easy way to say this, Mattie. I wish I could spare you this hurt."

"Shut up." Her voice was muffled against his shirt. "I don't want to hear anymore."

"You have to. Mattie, we can't go into a marriage with this terrible misunderstanding between us." He gentled her with his hands, smoothing her hair, caressing her back. "I love you, Mattie. We'll get through this together. Look at me."

She lifted her head. Her eyes were wide and frightened. And something else, Hunter thought. She looked lost, as if she were a little girl who had suddenly been deprived of everything she held dear. He bit back a curse. She needed his strength, not his anger.

"I don't know what your mother told you. I don't want to know. But I did nothing wrong, Mattie. I was never alone with her; I never touched her."

"Stop it!" she screamed. "My mother loved me. She would never make up a thing like that."

"Of course she loved you. The pictures don't deny that. They are merely evidence of a . . . warped mind . . . a sickness." He groped for the right words, hoping that instinct and love would guide him.

Mattie jerked herself free and stood up. "It's a lie. She didn't make it up. She wouldn't." White and shaking, she lifted her hand and smashed it into Hunter's face. "You *raped* her. And then you tried to blackmail

her with those filthy pictures. You despicable bastard."
She stormed across the room and picked up a vase.
With all the strength of her rage, she hurled it across
the room. It missed Hunter's head by a good three feet
and shattered beside the sofa.

He was on his feet, striding toward her. "Mattie.
Stop it. I won't let you do this to yourself."

"Get out! Get out! I never want to see you again as
long as I live."

He caught her arm. "I'm not going to leave you like
this."

"If you don't get your hands off me, I'll make you
sorry you ever heard the name Mattie Houston."

"Mattie. Don't do this to us."

"Us? *Us!*" Her voice was hoarse from shouting. "You
destroyed us with those pictures!" She hauled against
his iron grip. "Let me go."

"No, dammit."

Mattie was not Phillip Houston's granddaughter for
nothing. Her leg shot out in a snap kick to the groin.
As Hunter doubled over she ran to the sofa, grabbed
the envelope, and flew out the door. By that time she
was crying so hard, she could barely see.

"I hate you. I hate all of you." She ran down the
hallway and into the blessed emptiness of her bedroom. She slammed and locked her door, then fell across
the bed. Each sob was torn from the depths of a bruised
and battered spirit. She thought she might never be
while again.

The noise of their battle had roused Phillip from his
study. Grim-faced, he stood at the foot of the stairs
and watched Mattie's flight to her bedroom.

"I knew there'd be the devil to pay for this," he
muttered.

He waited for Hunter to come out of the music room.
The minutes ticked by. Nothing happened. The silence
made his skin crawl.

"Aunt Beulah's drawers. What's going on?"

He hurried up the stairs and banged on Mattie's door. "Mattie! Mattie!"

"Leave me alone, Papa."

He stood uncertainly in the hall, then marched into the music room. Hunter was still on the floor, groaning. And another two-thousand-dollar vase had been smashed, the twin to the one he'd broken earlier.

"Dammit, boy. What happened?"

"She kicked me." Hunter attempted to straighten up, and failed. "Where in the hell did she learn that?"

Phillip stifled a proud grin. "From me. I thought a little karate might come in handy. I see it did."

Hunter finally managed to sit up. He grimaced. "Couldn't you have taught her something else, like a nice kick in the shins?"

"She's got that killer's instinct. Just like me." He squatted beside Hunter and patted his arm. "Take it easy, boy. It'll be all right in a minute."

"I don't think I'll ever be the same. She's probably ruined our family."

Phillip chuckled. "It'll feel that way for a while. What happened in here, anyway?"

"I told her the truth. She took it harder than I thought she would."

"Mattie's like William; he never wanted to face an unpleasant truth. But she's tougher than he was. More like her grandmother. And me. She'll come around eventually. She's in her bedroom, having second thoughts right now, I'll vow."

"It took her ten years to forgive me. I don't plan to wait another ten. I'm going to resolve this matter tonight, even if I have to break down her door to do it." He stood up with the intention of carrying out his plan, but he was shaky on his feet, and the pain in his groin commanded his full attention. "Maybe I'll wait until tomorrow."

"Good idea. Let her sleep on it. Things always look better in the broad light of day." Phillip spoke with more confidence than he felt. He knew his granddaughter. She was stubborn. He looked up at Hunter's ashen face. "You need an escort home, boy?"

"I'll make it." Hunter walked slowly and painfully from the room.

After he'd gone, Phillip remained, trying to believe that everything would be all right. His rationale was that Hunter and Mattie loved each other too much to let another misunderstanding come between them. It made him feel better, but not a whole lot. He had the uneasy feeling that he and Mickey had meddled.

The broken pieces of the Chinese vase caught his eye. He walked over to them and gave one a vicious kick. "Never did like those damned vases, anyhow."

Nine

Mattie lifted herself on one elbow and stared at the
envelope. All the horror she had felt ten years before
flooded through her. She didn't need to look inside to
see the pictures; they were etched clearly in her memory. Hunter and her mother. Victoria's hands pinned
back. Forced sex.

Mattie clenched her teeth and tried to shut out the
ugliness. But she could still hear her mother's voice
telling the revolting story. . . .

"He came from behind. I didn't even see him until
he'd already grabbed me." Victoria's voice was shaking
as she fought back tears. "Look at that top picture,
Mattie. You can see how it was. . . . Mattie? Can't you,
darling?"

Mattie hated the pictures. She wished she'd never
seen them. She wished Victoria had never told her.
The pictures were blurred and out of focus as she
stared at them through her tears. Her mother kept
talking, talking, going on and on about Hunter. She
wanted to yell, *"Shut up!"* but a great lump of fear
closed her throat.

"He forced me into the tub," her mother continued. "I fought him. Believe me, darling. I used all my pitiful strength against that—that *monster* you decided to marry. But he's strong, Mattie. You know that. He's a big man. He tore my suit, crushed me against the side of the tub, forced himself on me. It was awful!"

Her mother's voice battered Mattie's soul. Everything that was bright and beautiful in her world came crashing down at her feet. "Hunter, Hunter," her mind screamed. "How could you have done this?"

"As if the awful defilement weren't enough, that slimy photographer tried to blackmail me with these pictures. They show as plain as day what happened. I just hope he didn't keep a set. You know how they love to follow me around, hiding in the bushes, taking pictures, making up stories for their sleazy magazines. Only, this time, they don't have to make up a story. It's all there in black and white. I just hope my poor William never finds out."

Her loud sob made Mattie look up. Her mother's beauty always reached out and grabbed her. Even in her anguish Victoria was beautiful, like one of Shakespeare's tragic heroines. No wonder Hunter couldn't keep his hands off her, she thought. A fresh stab of pain caught at Mattie.

"I . . . hate . . . him." Each word sliced her heart. She was breathless, drained, after she'd said them.

"I'm glad, darling," Victoria said. "I mean . . . I'm not glad it happened this way, but I'm happy you found out about him before you made the mistake of marrying him." She dabbed a perfume-scented handkerchief on her brow. "We won't tell your father, of course. There's no need for him to know what a rat his future son-in-law turned out to be. Poor William. He would be so heartbroken."

Mattie was numb. She could only nod her assent.

Victoria took the pictures from her and stuffed them back into the envelope. With a red felt-tip pen she scrawled "Private" across the left-hand corner of the envelope.

"Then it's settled, Mattie. You'll send the ring back. There's no need for you to ever see that wretch again."

"No. No need." Mattie managed to speak around the lump of fear in her throat, which was growing bigger and bigger. She felt cold and empty and frightened. Hunter had been her love, her friend, her strength. Who could she turn to now? Not her father. Her mother was right. No need for him to be hurt too. She couldn't even tell Papa. He had to live in Dallas, right next door to Hunter. There was no need to make it hard for him.

She longed to put her head on her mother's shoulder and cry, to feel her mother's arms around her, to know the comfort of being loved. But Victoria disliked overt displays of affection. Silly pampering, she called it. Mattie hugged her hurt to herself.

"We'll leave on the first plane out, darling." Victoria was suddenly gay. "We'll go on a lovely shopping spree as soon as we get to Europe. There's no better way to forget one's troubles than by spending money, lots of it. What do you say?"

Mattie said nothing. She was lost in her private hell. . . .

Mattie stared down at the envelope. It seemed to pulse with a strange power. She felt herself drawn to it, unable to keep from opening the flap, pulling out the hateful pictures.

"I won't look," she whispered. "Not my mother. Not my mother."

She shut her eyes against the pain that ripped through her. Memories flooded her mind. There was the day they had gone to the zoo. She recalled Victoria imitating the antics of the monkeys, the two of them laughing over the pink cotton candy that got all over their faces, and both of them riding an elephant, pretending to be on safari. And always, always Victoria had been beautiful. And somehow fragile. She had been so easy to love.

Her mother's charm had colored her childhood, had painted a bright aura of love around her. Even though Victoria had not been a toucher, she had convinced those around her of her love.

"Please, God, not Mommy." It was half plea, half prayer. In her agony Mattie used the name she'd called Victoria in the magic days of her childhood, the days when reality blended with fantasy and nothing bad existed in the world that a smile from her mother couldn't fix.

Mattie clenched her jaws and kept her eyes shut to the truth, clinging to her image of Victoria with the tenacity of a drowning sailor clinging to a sinking ship. But her hands refused to stuff the pictures back inside the envelope. Against her better judgment she opened her eyes and stared down at them. They were every bit as hideous as they had been ten years earlier. The only difference was that they weren't blurred through tears. She had no more tears to shed. She'd finished with crying over Hunter.

She bent over the photos, studying his profile, the broad shoulders, his black hair. That hair, she thought. Something wasn't right. She reached over and snapped on a bedside light. The dark hair of the man in the photograph was smooth, not tousled, like Hunter's.

She leaned closer. Something was wrong about the profile, as well. The chin was too sharp. And the shoulders . . . She could shut her eyes and see Hunter's shoulders. There was a subtle difference here, one she couldn't quite put a name to.

She fanned the pictures across the bedspread and looked at them from a different perspective. This time she didn't think about the physical evidence. She thought instead about the man, his tenderness, his humor, his honesty, his basic goodness.

Her hands shook as she gathered up the pictures and stuffed them back inside the envelope. Now she knew what had bothered her all these years. The pictures were out of character for Hunter. He was a straightforward, up-front man, with a strong sense of pride and nobility. He would never have forced himself on Victoria. He would never have betrayed Mattie with such a sneaky, vicious deed.

Her mind reeled. That meant Victoria had lied. Mattie tried to shut her mind to the thought, but the floodgate of possibilities was down. Little things spilled over—how Victoria had been caught crying when Mattie turned sixteen, how she'd always stayed around to charm Mattie's dates, how she'd been obsessed with the idea of remaining youthful.

Dazzling Victoria, with her harmless little flirtations; beautiful Victoria, with her charming mannerisms and her lilting laughter, had possessed a hard core of selfishness and deceit. How well she had hidden it. How easy it had been to believe in her beauty, her lies.

The truth lacerated Mattie's soul. The shock of it rocked the very foundations of her life. Her wedding, her happiness, her future with Hunter—all her bright dreams became obscure shadows, lifeless things, under the pall of darkness that fell over her spirit.

Hunter, she thought, her heart clenching with pain. She had a sudden vision of him—laughing, witty, tender, passionate. And then a second vision was superimposed over the first—Victoria, bright and beautiful and treacherous.

Mattie's hands tightened on the envelope. "Nooo!" she screamed. Then she was tearing and ripping and shredding, trying to rid herself of the awful truth by destroying the pictures.

When she had finished, she flung the pieces across the room and rose from the bed. Dry-eyed, she left her room in search of Papa. She found him downstairs, in his study.

"Papa."

"Mattie." He came to her swiftly and embraced her.

"I'm leaving, Papa. On the next flight to Paris."

"For how long, Mattie?"

"I don't know. I can't deal with this . . . this . . ." She waved her hand helplessly in the air. She couldn't bring herself to put an ugly label on what she had seen. Admitting it, saying it out loud, would simply make it so.

"Stay," Papa said. "I love you. Hunter loves you. The two of you can work it out."

She hesitated. Her need to see Hunter was so powerful, she could almost feel his arms around her. But if she went to him now, wounded and bleeding, if she sought refuge in his arms, it would be a betrayal of her mother, a denial of her childhood. Even worse, the rage she felt might be glossed over, sealed off. It would be only a temporary healing, a Band-Aid applied where major surgery was needed.

"I can't deal with anybody's feelings except my own, Papa."

He leaned back and looked into her face. "You're sure? I think running away would be a mistake."

"I'm not running away this time. I'm making a rational decision to separate myself from everybody and everything that reminds me of my mother's selfishness."

"What about Hunter? It seems that he's the most maligned one in this sorry business."

"I'll call him."

"I'm glad for that much, at least." Papa patted her shoulder and chuckled. "He might not be so glad to hear from you, though. Your aim is lethal. I taught you well."

She kissed his cheek. "You're a rock, Papa. What would I do without you?"

"No need to find out. I'm planning to set a record for longevity."

"Is that a promise?"

"It's a promise."

Back upstairs Mattie made two calls: one to an airline and one to Hunter. The first was easy, the second hard.

"I'm flying back to Paris, Hunter—"

"Dammit, Mattie—"

"—tomorrow."

Hunter felt as if an anvil had been dropped on his heart. Common sense told him that she needed time to reconcile herself to the truth, but his gut reaction was to rush next door and keep her in Dallas, to make her face the truth. Squelching that urge, he made himself ask a sensible question.

"When are you coming back?"

"I don't know."

"I can't let you go like this. You need me. We need each other."

"I need . . ." She hesitated, thinking about what she needed. She needed Hunter, his love, his strength, his encouragement. But she also needed her mother. She needed something, some bright and wonderful image, to fill the great, aching void inside her. "I need nobody," she finished. "I need time."

"We need to talk. We can resolve this problem together."

"I'm finished with talking. I may even be finished with thinking. All I want is to be alone."

Hunter was afraid. He recognized an old pattern. Mattie hated to face an unpleasant truth, had always hated it. She would run to the ends of the earth to preserve her blindness. He clenched his jaw so hard he nearly cracked a tooth.

"I'd come over there right now," he said, "and chain you to the bed if I thought it would keep you here . . . and if I could move. Damn. You kick like a mule."

"Save your energy for something else . . . somebody else."

"Mattie . . ."

"I've suddenly discovered that I don't have what it takes to sustain a relationship."

"If you think for one minute I'm going to let you go . . . Mattie?" Hunter was talking to a dead receiver.

• • •

Mattie set Paris on its ear. At the Moulin Rouge she climbed onstage, kicked off her shoes, and did glissandos on the piano with her bare feet. Her entourage of doting men carried her around the room on a huge silver platter, borrowed from the waiter. She attended a costume party dressed as a musical note. The black sequined note, attached to a sheer body suit, barely covered her strategic parts. An enterprising photographer got a by-line on the front page with her picture.

Her behavior kept her in the headlines. And her fear kept her running. She lived high and fast. She spent time and money as freely as if neither would ever run out. She didn't look forward and she didn't look back. Rather, she lived for the moment. She surrounded herself with people—gay, frivolous people who wouldn't ask her to think. She attended parties, she gave parties, and she played cards with a vengeance.

In just two weeks she won and lost enough at the poker table to outfit a twelve-man safari to Africa. In one of her moments of intense gaiety she even planned the safari.

But in the still, lonesome moments of the night, those dark hours after midnight when she had no one to love, her fears haunted her. She was afraid of facing the truth about the mother she'd loved, the woman she'd thought was wonderful, the woman she'd sought to emulate. She knew she had Victoria's gaiety and lilting laughter. Did she also have her cold, devious heart? she wondered. Did she have a hidden core of selfishness that would someday surface? She was flesh of Victoria's flesh, heart of her heart. Did that mean the old adage would come true? Like mother like daughter? Not only her future, but her very identity, was threatened.

And so, in order to keep her identity intact, Mattie invented her mother. She closed her eyes to a part of the truth, shutting out all that was bad, and concentrated on the bright moments of her youth. She conjured up the carrousel rides and the birthday pony and the summer picnics. She created for herself an ordinary mother, one she could love . . . and imitate.

The first week Mattie was gone, Hunter was reasonable and sensible and mature. He told himself that he would give her the time she needed, that he would cope with her absence by staying busy. He jogged till his legs threatened to buckle and swam till his arms were too heavy to move. He spent so much time at work, Uncle Mickey accused him of sleeping at the office.

The second week was harder. He began to put salt in his coffee and catsup in his cereal. He took to muttering to himself, and he had all-night marathons of cartoon watching.

Uncle Mickey complained that a body couldn't get a decent night's sleep for the racket from Bugs Bunny. He claimed if he heard that rabbit scream, "What's up, Doc?" one more time in the middle of the night, he'd personally shoot the VCR.

But the final indignity came when Hunter put the newspaper in the washing machine with Uncle Mickey's favorite, peppermint-striped pajamas.

"You've ruined them," Uncle Mickey said, holding up his pitiful pajamas. Their once-proud stripes were blackened with printer's ink. Bits of gooey paper clung to them. "They look like they have smallpox."

"Sorry," Hunter said. "I had my mind on other things."

"Mattie."

"Yes."

"When's she coming back?"

"I don't know. I haven't heard from her."

"Then what are you doing, sitting here in Dallas? Get your butt on a plane to Paris before we all go crazy."

Hunter did exactly that. The first thing he saw after he landed in Paris was a picture of Mattie, wearing a policeman's hat and a bikini hardly big as a handker-chief, directing traffic on the Boulevard des Capucines.

He grinned. "At least she's not moping."

It took him exactly forty minutes to get from the airport to Mattie's apartment.

When her doorbell rang, Mattie was sitting in a tub-ful of bubbles. "Bother," she muttered as she stepped out of the tub. Without pausing for a wrap, she ran to the front door, leaving a trail of soap bubbles. "Who-ever you are, go away," she called through the door. "I'm not receiving callers today."

"I'm not a caller, Mattie. I'm your future husband."

Excitement exploded in her. She put her hand on the door chain, then pulled it back. Damn, she thought. She wasn't ready to face Hunter. And she certainly wasn't ready to face a future. Right now she was living for the moment.

"Go away, Hunter."

"Mattie." He rattled the doorknob. "Let me in."

"No."

He stood outside her apartment considering his op-tions. He could kick the door down, but that wouldn't remedy her stubbornness. He could stand here and keep pestering her, hoping she would relent, but that wasn't his style. Suddenly he smiled. He had always preferred a flamboyant approach, and what he had in mind should send her barriers tumbling. It might even send her scurrying for cover.

"This is war, Mattie," he said through the door. "Get ready to have your citadels penetrated."

She couldn't help but grin. "Whatever happened to my door to paradise?"

She waited and listened, but there was no reply. Finally she looked through the peephole. Hunter was no longer there.

Hunter didn't waste any time. He hired a private

detective that day, and every move Mattie made was reported to him.

"She's attending the opera tonight," Claude Lévêque told him the next morning. "Mozart's *Don Giovanni.* Her escort is Jean-Louis Rameau. He has a box at the Opéra." Claude, a fastidious little man, wiped a bead of perspiration from his moustache, carefully refolded his immaculate handkerchief, and continued his report. "Jean-Louis is curator at the National Museum of Modern Art. He's forty-four, a widower, and has two grown children and six cats. He drives a black BMW, license number 78564. This is a snapshot of him entering the museum." He handed Hunter the picture.

"Skinny devil," Hunter commented. "What in the world does she see in him?"

"He's rich, old family money. And he has quite a reputation with the ladies. Smooth, fast-talking, a veritable—"

"That was a rhetorical question. I don't want to hear about his bedroom exploits." He took the report from Claude. "Good work. There's no need for you to follow her tonight. I'll be with her."

"Shall I expect to resume trailing the lady tomorrow morning?"

He hoped not, Hunter thought. Tomorrow morning he expected to be occupying the lady's bed. "I'll call you if I need you again."

When Mattie came out the front door of her apartment building, Hunter felt as if a Roman candle had exploded inside him. Her sheer French silk gown fit like sin on a fallen angel. It was green, like her eyes. The satin underdress left so much skin bare, it must have been an afterthought. Diamantés, attached to sheer chiffon, were sprinkled over her arms and shoulders, beckoning across the hot night to him. Her glorious hair, caught high in an emerald clip, cascaded down her shoulders.

It took all his willpower to keep from running across the street and snatching her out of Jean-Louis Rameau's clutches. That shriveled-up little Romeo didn't deserve to be breathing the same air as Mattie, Hunter thought as the enamored Frenchman tucked her into his car.

Hunter followed boldly along, even tailgating on occasion. That smitten Frenchman wouldn't have noticed if a military parade were in his wake, he figured. Who would, with the intoxicating Mattie at his side?

Hunter parked near them and waited until they had entered the Opéra. Then he approached the black BMW. The Frenchman had been careless. The doors weren't even locked. Stealing his car was going to be easy.

Hunter hot-wired the car and drove off. He chuckled all the way to the police station. Leaving the car parked right outside the door, he walked inside the station and used the pay phone to call the Opéra.

"Please bring Monsieur Jean-Louis Rameau to the phone. Urgent police business." He hoped his French didn't sound as awful to the theater manager as it did to himself.

While he waited he imagined the cocky little Frenchman's hand on Mattie's knee. He pictured that hand creeping boldly up her skirt. By the time Jean-Louis picked up the receiver, Hunter hated him.

Jealousy helped disguise the southern brogue that kept filtering into his terrible French.

"This is Inspector Duvalier. We've recovered your stolen vehicle."

"My car hasn't been stolen. It's parked in the lot at the Opéra. Who are you and how did you know where to find me?"

"Your housekeeper informed me where you were. Is your license number 78564?"

"Yes! Impossible!"

Hunter grinned. The little man actually squeaked when he talked. He hoped he had warts, too. On his private parts. "We require your presence at the police station in the ninth *arrondissement.*"

"I cannot leave now. I'm with a woman."

The rush of blood to his brain obscured Hunter's vision. "Immediately!"

"I'll be there in twenty minutes."

Hunter smiled with satisfaction as he hung up. With Jean-Louis out of the way, he now had Mattie to attend to. As his cab hurtled through the dark streets toward the Opéra, he thought he saw the Frenchman's cab going the other way.

Intermission was just ending when he slipped into the empty seat beside Mattie. Thinking Jean-Louis had changed his mind and come back, she turned around.

"It's you!" she exclaimed. The expression on her face was a mixture of exasperation and amusement.

"An improvement, don't you think?" He spread his long legs so his thigh was touching hers.

Mattie glanced at the adjoining boxes. She was certain their stage whispers were disrupting the entire theater. She needn't have been concerned. The rollicking scene onstage had completely captivated the audience's attention. "You can't stay here," she whispered fiercely.

He tucked a curl behind her ear. "Don't worry, princess. I plan to adjourn to your apartment as quickly as possible." He leaned over and kissed the tender spot next to the curl.

"Jean-Louis is waiting for me in my apartment."

"Jean-Louis is at the police station. He'll be busy for quite a while, trying to find the policeman who reported his car stolen." He chuckled.

"*You* stole his car?"

"It's one of my many talents." He started massaging the back of her neck. "Do you want to see the rest of them?"

"You ought to be arrested."

"I probably would be if the police knew what I was thinking." He nibbled her ear. "You want to see the rest of my talents, Mattie?"

"Stop that. You're ruining the opera."

"I'm hoping to ruin our reputations." He pulled the emerald clip from her hair, which he let cascade over his arm. "I'd like to walk barefoot through your hair."

"I'd like to do something else with my bare foot."

"I love it when you're angry. Your eyes glitter like cat's eyes." He twisted a strand of her shining hair around his hand. "You're a luscious cat, Mattie."

Mattie had thought she could endure his preposterous remarks. She'd thought she could watch the rest of the opera and then leave with dignity, leave Hunter sitting there wishing he'd never come. But she couldn't. His presence brought back all the things she was trying to forget—their love, their promises, her mother's betrayal. He weakened her resolve to live for the moment and made her question her decision to deal with hurt by pretending it didn't exist. She'd thought she could come to Paris and live a carefree life, not making commitments, not forming attachments.

She turned to face him. He was so heart-stoppingly gorgeous, he made her lose her breath. He wore his tuxedo and his charm with such careless grace, he might have invented them both. Oh, Hunter, she thought. *Why did you come here? Why couldn't you let me go?*

He seemed to be reading her thoughts. He smiled, and that, too, was devastating. She stood up, dumping her program onto the floor.

"I'm leaving."

"Good."

He matched her stride for stride as she left the box. She turned on him. "Go away."

"Never. You once told me never to let you forget that you love me. I'm keeping that promise."

"I don't want to hear it. I can't deal with it right now."

"If you don't deal with it now, you never will."

"Leave me alone." She lifted her skirts and drew back a lethal leg.

"Mattie!" He was too fast for her. Before she'd aimed her kick, he scooped her up and slung her over his shoulder.

She pounded his back. "Put me down."

"Only if you promise to behave."

"Never!"

They attracted more than a little attention as they left the theater. She was a celebrity and he was devilishly handsome. A few of Mattie's fans, who took great delight in following all her escapades, remarked that it looked as if she had met her match.

They encountered one reluctant patron of the arts in the lobby. He blocked Hunter's path.

"Excush me. Ish that caterwauling finish?"

Mattie took the opportunity to bite Hunter's butt. She took a hefty mouthful, tuxedo and all.

"Dammit!" he yelled.

"My shentiments, exshactly. Wife made me come."

"It's not over yet," Hunter told him. "Now, if you'll excuse me, I have to get the wife home. She's dead on her feet." He patted Mattie's backside.

She kicked his thigh.

The man seemed to notice Mattie for the first time. "Shay. How'd she get up there?"

"She climbed. Can't keep her off me. She's wild about me."

Mattie retaliated by pinching his leg.

He swatted her butt. "She's a regular little hellcat."

The man reeled aside, laughing. "Marsha won't believe thish. The besh show wash in the lobby."

Hunter strode out the door and to the parking lot. He didn't put Mattie down until he got to his car. Opening the door with one hand, he dumped her onto the front seat.

"This is kidnapping, you bully."

"Remember what happened the last time I kidnapped you? You loved it, Mattie."

"I'll open the window and scream."

"With your reputation, nobody will pay any attention."

She knew that was true. Besides, nobody would bother to involve himself in her affairs. That was one of the things she'd always loved about Paris: People minded their own business.

As Hunter whizzed through the streets toward her apartment, she clung to her indignation, hoping it would insulate her against the powerful attraction she felt for Hunter.

"You can bulldoze your way into my apartment," she said when they reached her building. "You can hug me, you can kiss me, you can even have your way with me—"

He roared with laughter. "Such an old-fashioned term coming from such a modern day hellcat."

"It's not funny, Hunter. Stop laughing."

Suddenly he was serious. He reached over and covered her hand with his. "If I don't keep laughing I'm liable to cry, Mattie. I'm not going to let you pretend that I don't exist."

"I'm not pretending."

"Yes, you are. It seems to be the only way you can deal with what your mother did."

She covered her ears. "I don't want to hear it."

Hunter felt a cold shiver of defeat. He'd hoped to avoid this subject until he had Mattie back in his arms. He'd hoped to rebuild trust and love with affection. He'd planned to show her that she could turn to him, even with this problem. "You've got to face it sometime, Mattie," he said quietly.

"I can't. I can't deal with anything except how I feel."

"How do you feel?"

"Empty. Betrayed. Used."

"I'm here for you. Lean on me, Mattie."

"No." She clenched her hands and glared at him. "Don't you understand? You remind me too much of what she did. Every time I see you, I think of her treachery." She pounded her hands on his shoulder. "I hate her. I hate my own mother. Nobody can change that."

"I understand your rage. And I'm glad you can vent some of it on me." He parked the car in front of her apartment and turned to look at her. "My shoulders are broad; they can take a pounding." He grinned. "As long as you stay away from the family jewels."

"I'm sorry about that, Hunter. Did it hurt much?"

"Not any more than if King Kong had used me for a volleyball." He pulled her into his arms. He could feel the tension in her stiff back and unyielding shoulders. "We need each other, Mattie. Your rage will pass, and when it does, I want to be there at your side."

His tenderness almost penetrated her shell of resolve. She was almost persuaded that there was still room in her heart for love. But the images of those damning pictures burned through her memory, and she knew there wasn't. Rage consumed her. Each day she woke up to the searing knowledge that she hated her own mother. The only way she could endure such knowledge was to live on the cutting edge of excitement, live as if nothing mattered but selfish pursuits in a cruel world.

She pushed against his shoulder. "No, Hunter."

"I won't let you go."

He kissed her swiftly, before she could turn away. Everything about the kiss was tender—the gentle touch of his lips, the sweet coaxing of his tongue, even the way he held her. The kiss gave everything and demanded nothing. Because of that, she couldn't turn away. She leaned into him. She felt safe. She felt protected. For the moment, she gave herself up to the haven of Hunter's arms.

The kiss lasted until her bones had turned to liquid, until the imprint of him was tattooed on her heart. It lasted until he had almost mounted the battlements of her hurt and penetrated the citadels of her pretense. It lasted until there was no air left in the hot car to breathe.

He pulled back and looked down at her. "I need you, Mattie. We need each other."

"No. Don't you understand? I can't love and hate at the same time."

"You don't have to. Just *be*, and let time heal your wounds."

All the hatred—and the love—she felt for her mother burst inside her, and she pushed Hunter away.

"Go home, Hunter."

"No."

"I have to deal with this my way."

"Your way excludes me. I won't be left out of your life, Mattie. Not for a few weeks, not for a few days, not even for a few hours."

"You have no choice. My door is closed to you."

"Your apartment door or your door to paradise?"

He smiled at her. It was a smile of such charm, such persuasion, that she almost fell back into his arms.

"Both," she said.

He caught her hands. "I'm not asking for any promises. I'm not asking that you keep any appointed schedule. I'm simply asking that you let me be a part of your life. I want to share your pain as well as your joy."

"Words. Those are just pretty words, Hunter." She pulled her hands away. "I know about pretty words. My mother was a master of them."

"Dammit, Mattie. I'm not your mother. Those are not just pretty words." He caught her shoulders. "I love you. Nothing's going to change that."

"Can't you see? There's too much inside me now, too much pain and ugliness. I can't give you what you want. I can't be anything to you."

"I'm not asking that you *give*, Mattie. Not right now. I'm asking you to *receive*. I want you to accept my support."

"No. I have to be free. I don't want any reminders of

the past." She put her hand on the door handle. "Go back to Dallas, Hunter, where you belong."

"I belong wherever you are. And that's how it's going to be. You won't get rid of me that easily. I'm not Jean-Louis Rameau."

His stubbornness suddenly made her angry. Why couldn't he see things her way? If he loved her so, why didn't he respect her wishes? In her confusion and ire she reached for the most effective weapon she knew, a brittle, woman-of-the-world facade.

"How do you know I planned to get rid of Jean-Louis? I hear he's quite talented in bed."

Hunter's eyes turned blacker than sin. "Don't start that game with me."

She shoved open the door and stepped onto the sidewalk. Bending over, she made her parting shot. "Maybe it's no game. Maybe I'm proving the old adage: like mother, like daughter."

"You're not Victoria!"

She didn't bother to reply. She didn't even bother to close the car door. She turned and walked quickly into her apartment building. The slam of the door resounded through the sultry summer night.

The veins stood out in Hunter's neck. As he leaned across the seat to shut his car door, a small poodle passed by.

"What are you grinning at?" Hunter shouted. "There's not a damn thing funny around here."

The poor, frightened dog tucked his manicured tail in and raced down the street.

While most of Paris slept, two restless people paced their floors. Mattie thought of Victoria's betrayal and kicked her vanity. Hunter thought of Mattie's stubbornness and struck his desk. Mattie remembered the feel of Hunter's arms and hugged her pillow. Hunter remembered the taste of Mattie's lips and gazed out the window.

"I'll be so wicked, he'll go back to Dallas in disgust," Mattie told the walls of her apartment. "Then I'll be free."

"I'll be so persistent, she won't be able to shut me out," Hunter told the walls of his hotel room. "Then we'll be happy."

Having come to those conclusions, the star-crossed lovers climbed into their separate beds.

Ten

"When will you be back, Hunter?"

The long-distance line crackled, and Hunter held the receiver away from his ear before answering.

"Not until I settle this thing with Mattie, Uncle Mickey."

"Katz has doubled its order for skater babies but wants them all by Thanksgiving. Our new ad director is chomping at the bit because he can't go ahead on the new campaign without your okay. Our assembly line is chaotic, with all those new designs going through, and a woman named Kathleen Forbes Clynton is worrying your secretary to a frazzle trying to locate you."

Hunter glared at the receiver as if it were responsible for all the bad news. "Get Kurt down to the assembly line to straighten that out. I'll call him about hiring new people to handle the Katz order. Air-express the ad campaign to me and I'll handle it here. Tell Kathleen my tennis-racket injury is permanent."

Uncle Mickey laughed. "That ought to stop her. By the way, Janet and I are getting married."

"That's great! Congratulations."

"We're thinking of honeymooning in the giant boy tox. I introduced her to it last night. It's become her favorite place."

Hunter hooted with laughter. "I'd have the thing air-expressed to Paris if I thought it would work with Mattie."

"She's still being stubborn, huh?"

"And hurt. But she's so damned independent, she won't let me help her. She won't even let me near her."

"Do you have a plan?"

"I always have a plan."

After he'd hung up, Hunter gazed at the latest report from Claude Lévêque. Mattie would be attending a house party this weekend at Jean-Louis Rameau's country estate, just outside Paris. Plans included a costume party, a scavenger hunt, and horse racing.

A couple of quick phone calls got him an invitation to the Rameau estate. The dangerous glint in his black eyes signaled that he was plotting devilment.

Mattie's bare feet sank into the plush carpet as she unpacked her clothes in one of Jean-Louis's guest rooms. She smiled when she hung up her costume. The shock of it should keep Paris talking for months. Hunter would read about it in the papers. Maybe it would send him flying back to Dallas.

Her smile faded. Was that what she really wanted? she asked herself. To send the man she loved out of her life forever? Not really. But at the moment it seemed the best solution.

She closed the closet door and went downstairs to lunch.

Everybody agreed that Jean-Louis had outdone himself. The costume party was one of the most elaborate he'd ever had. But where was Mattie Houston? they asked. There were belly dancers and Indians and pirates and alligators and devils, and there was even a zebra. But where was Mattie?

Hunter was wondering the same thing. He stood in

the crowded ballroom beside a marble column, trying to keep his sword from spearing the backside of a ridiculous fat man in an alligator suit. He was terribly hot in his pirate's garb, and wished he'd chosen to be primitive rather than swashbuckling. A loincloth would have felt good in this heat. He reached up and loosened the tie on his green cape. The damned thing was choking him to death.

Suddenly a murmur ran through the crowd and everybody turned toward the French doors.

"It's a horse!" someone shouted.

"It's Lady Godiva!"

"It's Mattie Houston!"

Mattie rode the white horse sidesaddle. His hooves clattered on the marble floor as she pranced him right through the middle of the crowd. The room was so still, a falling snowflake would have made a loud crash, for Mattie was wearing nothing except a flesh-colored body suit, a long blond wig, and a smile.

The alligator poked his snout into Hunter's face.

"That woman's got guts," he said. "Nobody's pulled a stunt like that since Eleanor of Aquitaine rode naked to the Crusades."

"She's remarkable, all right."

"She has quite a reputation, you know." The man's fat lips drooled into his alligator teeth. "I think I'll go over there and try my luck with her."

Hunter stepped forward and planted his boot on the alligator's tail. When the man moved, he lost the whole backside of his costume with a great tearing sound.

"What the devil . . . ?"

"I think you just lost your tail," Hunter said. "Better go upstairs and make repairs."

He chuckled as the man waddled off, his round behind heaving to and fro in his exposed red boxer shorts.

The Indian next to Hunter laughed. "I saw what you did. The pompous old geezer deserved every bit of it. He's a fortune hunter."

"I never did trust a man who wears boxer shorts,"

Hunter said. He left the Indian, to fight his way through the crowd that surrounded Mattie.

The instant the broad-shouldered pirate stepped into her circle of admirers, Mattie knew it was Hunter. Even if his untamed hair hadn't given him away, the fierce black eyes would have. They fairly sizzled behind his mask.

She tried to still the jackhammer rhythm of her heart as she unconsciously smoothed the long wig over her breasts.

Hunter caught the horse's bridle. "If it isn't the shocking Miss Mattie Houston," he drawled.

His voice made shivers crawl up her legs. The horse sensed her excitement and danced nervously in place.

"Do I shock you, Hunter?" she asked.

"On the contrary. You delight me."

The group of admirers sensed that something private was going on between Lady Godiva and the big pirate. They gathered their feathered fans and broadswords and side arms and faded into the background.

"I thought you wanted a sweet, innocent woman," Mattie said.

"Sweet and innocent, sinful and wicked. I don't give a damn, Mattie." He moved closer, so that he could caress her leg. "I want whatever you are. You can take that ridiculous wig off and parade stark naked through the streets of Paris, for all I care. I'd be waiting to apply the sunburn lotion when you got off the horse."

In spite of his words, Mattie clung stubbornly to the notion that she could drive him away if only she were wicked enough.

"You haven't seen anything yet," she said. "Jean-Louis's parties get really raunchy. I'll probably throw this wig in the fountain and swing from the chandelier before the night's over."

"I'll be in a front-row seat, applauding. I love a feisty woman."

She was not deterred. "Have you ever seen anybody dance wearing a Lady Godiva wig? It's hell keeping all that hair in the right places."

"Don't you have to get off the horse first?" He reached up and circled her waist under all the Dynel hair. "Let me help you down, Mattie."

"Don't you dare."

She kicked her heels into the horse's flank, and the horse lunged forward. She felt Hunter's grip loosen, felt the bump of his chest against her horse as she plunged into the crowd.

"Look out!" she yelled as she bore down on the zebra. The front of the zebra went north and the back went south as she surged between them. The horse was nervous in the crowd, and she hadn't ridden in three years. She crushed Tarzan's stuffed ape, squashed an Indian's peace pipe, and nearly crashed into the champagne fountain before she could get the horse to stop.

"Nice going, Mattie," Jean-Louis said, appearing at her side. "I can always count on you to keep a party good and lively."

"Thanks." She gathered the reins tightly and glanced back over her shoulder to see how Hunter was taking her departure. He wasn't there. She looked around the room, trying to spot the black-haired pirate. He was nowhere to be seen. Puzzled, she turned her attention back to her host.

Mattie would have needed X-ray vision to see Hunter. He was upstairs making a drastic costume change. He stood in his room, gloriously naked, wielding a huge pair of scissors he'd found in the Louis XIV desk.

"She wants me to be shocked, does she?" he muttered. "I'll show her shocking.'"

He held up the remains of his green pirate's cape.

"Not bad."

He measured it for size.

"Just about right."

He tied his costume in place and inspected it in the pier mirror, then laughed at the ridiculous figure he cut.

"A little too much ventilation."

As he pondered the problem, he remembered seeing

a tipsy sixteenth-century French courtier in the hallway. He stepped outside and caught the man just as he was entering a bedroom down the hall.

"I need to borrow your tights," Hunter said.

The man lurched against the wall and inspected Hunter. "You cher-tain-ly do." He tugged on Hunter's arm. "Here, man." He stripped off the tights and handed them to Hunter. "I won't be needing theshe much longer anyhow."

Hunter returned to his bedroom, pulled on the pale tights, and went downstairs grinning.

His entrance was not as dramatic as Mattie's, but it certainly didn't go unnoticed. A white-haired woman in a pink Barbara Cartland costume dropped her champagne glass.

"Great Caesar's ghost!" she said. "Where'd you get that big . . . fig leaf?"

"Texas. Everything grows big in Texas."

The people who had been alerted by the shattering of the champagne glass heard the exchange and roared with laughter. That sound caught Mattie's attention. She carefully made her way toward the source.

She nearly fell off her horse when she saw Hunter. Two very nicely shaped, very big fig leaves were tied, front and back, over his groin and butt. Except for the tights, which left little to the imagination, the rest of him was as gorgeously naked as if he'd stepped from the shower. Her chuckle started as a smile and grew into a gale of laughter that made her double over the horse's mane.

Hunter was immediately beside her.

"Are you ready to dance now, Mattie?"

She sat up and wiped tears of laughter off her cheeks. "Dance? Are you crazy?"

"You wanted to be shocking." He pulled her off the horse. "I'm helping you out."

Her heavy wig tipped dangerously, exposing her right breast. Even through her body suit Hunter could see the dusky rose nipple, hardened to a peak. The amber light glittered in his eyes.

Mattie studied his face as she hastily readjusted her false hair. He looked as stubborn as she felt. Furthermore, he was gripping her waist in a way that said he had no intention of letting go.

She rebounded in typical Mattie fashion.

Wrapping her arms around his neck, she whispered into his ear, "Do you want to see what I can do to a fig leaf?"

"If it's more than Eve did in the garden, I'm in trouble."

She pressed closer to him. Her false hair and his fig leaf were no protection for the erotic friction that threatened to send them up in flames.

"One more move like that," he said, "and the front of this costume will be airborne."

He pulled her tightly against him and led her smoothly into a dance to the slow, sultry music.

"Jazz," he murmured against her hair. "It always reminds me of you."

Being in his arms made her forgetful. Nothing could ever go wrong in Hunter's arms, she thought. She wished the music would never stop. She wished the night would never end.

Her breasts were crushed against his chest, and his hands were caressing her back under the mass of false hair. She was stunningly aware of their scanty attire. As they danced, desire spiraled through her so fiercely, her knees would have buckled if Hunter hadn't been holding her so tightly. She had to trust her natural sense of rhythm to get her through the dance, for her mind had ceased to function.

"What's the name of this song, Mattie?"

" 'Can't Help Lovin' Dat Man.' "

"Does it last two or three hours?"

"No. Why?"

"It's going to be that long before I can get this fig leaf to behave."

She knew he wasn't joking. Judging from the insistent pressure, they'd have to do something soon or they'd be making love on the dance floor. A hank of hair and a scrap of material wouldn't be enough to keep them apart. "Just keep dancing, Hunter."

He chuckled softly. "I love it when you're breathless, Mattie."

"I am not."

"Yes, you are. It reminds me of the night we decided to go for a moonlight swim. Remember that game of water tag we started? Remember how I pulled you under? The way it felt with nothing between us and our desire except our wet swimsuits?"

She remembered. It had been near the beginning of the summer, when their awareness of each other had been so keen that every glance, every movement, every word, had been magnified.

Yes, she remembered. And it did feel the same. She'd wanted him to take her then, just as she wanted it now, wanted it with such a fierceness, she wished everybody in the room would disappear in a poof of smoke.

She closed her eyes and leaned her head against his shoulder.

"Keep dancing, Hunter," she whispered. "Don't let the music stop."

"I won't."

They danced through two sets and one intermission, never letting go. They might have solved their problems simply by holding each other if it hadn't been for the horse.

Suddenly Mattie came out of her dreamlike trance. "Good grief. My horse just took a bite of Helen Montague's grass skirt."

"I noticed some time back that she needed tying."

"Helen or the horse?"

"Both. The horse was nibbling Julius Caesar's wig and Helen was nibbling his . . . canapés."

Mattie was grateful for Hunter's easy wit. It helped dispel some of the mesmerizing power of his presence. She pulled out of his arms.

"I think the music has ended, Hunter."

She glanced around the room for the horse, for Jean-Louis, for anything that would take her attention away from Hunter.

"You told me not to let it stop," he said.

His hand cupped her chin, forcing her to look up. She caught her breath. Being in the path of those eyes was like being in a steam bath, she thought. And the sooner she got out, the sooner she'd be saved from a heat stroke.

"Did I say that, Hunter? It was temporary madness. Jean-Louis's parties always affect me that way."

"Don't do that, Mattie."

"What?"

"Pretend. I'm the man you love, and you keep pretending that I don't exist." He caught her hands and rubbed them across his bare chest. "Feel that, Mattie. I'm real. I exist. All the pretense in the world won't make me vanish."

"I don't want you to vanish. I just want you to go back to Dallas and leave me alone."

"Is that really what you want?"

Her hands trembled on his chest. The beat of his heart sounded like the march of time. Each stroke ticked off another irretrievable moment. Each pulse marked an empty interval without the man she loved.

She hesitated. Was she making a mistake? she wondered. Was pushing him away the answer to her problems? She wished she had the gift of foresight. She wished she had his confidence that time would heal her wounds. But at the moment all she had were a set of jumbled emotions and not enough feelings to go around. In order to survive, she had to be stingy. She had to protect her spirit. She couldn't afford to expend emotions on Hunter or anybody else. Getting through one day at a time was her main objective at the moment.

"Go," she said. The word was barely a whisper, and she hoped it would be effective.

He lifted her hands to his lips. His piercing eyes saw the lie.

"I'll go," he said. "For now."

As she watched him walk away she thought that he was the only man alive who could make a fig leaf look dignified. With that magnificent, burnished body he could have walked across the ballroom stark naked and made everybody else feel overdressed.

Hunter had class—and she was letting him go. A sudden panic seized her, and she opened her mouth to call him back. But something stopped her. Call it pride, call it cowardice, call it fear. Whatever it was, it stilled her cry. The moment was lost. Hunter disappeared from the ballroom, and Mattie went in search of her horse.

The way Hunter sat on a horse should be declared illegal, Mattie decided. She tried to pay attention to Jean-Louis. She tried to care about what he was saying. But she couldn't keep her eyes off Hunter. In their skintight jeans, his muscular legs hugged the black stallion's sides. His bronzed chest, bared by the unbuttoned white shirt, gleamed in the sunlight and looked as powerful as the horse he rode.

Three other riders were lined up beside him, waiting for the race to begin, but in Mattie's eyes there was only Hunter. She was sitting in the end seat of the fifth row, and she nearly fell off trying to get a better view.

Jean-Louis stood up and walked to the microphone. "Gentlemen, select your colors."

Mattie watched as the three other riders rode up to the bleachers. Three eager women came forward and tied their scarves around the riders' upper arms. Hunter remained at the starting line.

Jean-Louis spoke into the microphone once more. "Select your colors."

A smile of pure devilment lit Hunter's face as he nudged his horse forward. With the nonchalance of a postman picking up the mail, he rode up to the bleachers and scooped Mattie into his arms. Pressed tightly to his body, she felt as if she'd tumbled into an inferno.

Jean-Louis was not pleased. "I said, select your colors."

Hunter settled her into the saddle in front of him and stroked her hair. "These are my colors."

She felt branded. His hand on her hair, his chest against her back, his groin pressing into her hips, his legs brushing hers—all were forever imprinted on her. Her breathing became rapid. She wondered why Paris in the summertime had never been this scorching before.

"You can't race with her in the saddle," Jean-Louis said. "The extra weight will handicap you. You'll never win."

"I'll take my chances," Hunter said as he walked the horse back to the starting line.

"This is insanity," Mattie said.

"This is brilliant," Hunter told her.

Jean-Louis's face was tight as he glanced once more at his determined guest. "You know the rules," he said into the microphone. "Cross country. The course is well marked. No shortcuts. No using the crop. May the best man win."

"You'll never win like this, you know," Mattie told Hunter.

He tightened his arms around her. "I've already won."

The starting gun sounded, and Mattie felt the black stallion lunge forward. The wind whipped her hair back from her face as they galloped past the other three riders. The big stallion was powerful, and he soon outdistanced the other horses.

As they raced across the open fields and into the woods, Mattie realized that Hunter wasn't pacing the horse. He was giving him his head. Suddenly they veered off the marked course. Low-hanging branches impeded their progress, and Hunter reined the stallion down to a trot.

"This is not the course," Mattie said.

He chuckled. "It's the course I've planned."

"You don't even know where you are. We'll get lost."

"I paid Jean-Louis's stable boy a handsome sum to

give me a private tour of the estate. We'll be lost only as long as I want us to be."

"You should have been a pirate, Hunter. Kidnapping is your style."

He laughed. "I thought you came willingly."

"I did *not.*"

"You slid into this saddle as if you'd been waiting for the chance."

"You're an arrogant cad, Hunter."

"That's what you love about me, isn't it, Mattie?"

She ignored the remark and concentrated on the scenery. It was easy to do. The woods on Jean-Louis's estate were lush and well cared-for. Clean-cut riding trails wound through the forest. Here and there sunlight filtered through the thick trees, illuminating patches of yellow and purple wild flowers.

Hunter reined to a stop beside a small stream. He slid from the saddle and smiled up at Mattie.

"Are you coming, princess?"

"Why are we stopping?"

"Can't you guess?"

"I don't even want to try. I want to go back to the house."

"Not yet." He reached up and plucked her from the saddle. "First this."

With the swiftness of a nighthawk, his lips crushed down on hers. Her mouth parted to receive his tongue. She was willing. She was eager. She was flame. Nothing was heard in the silent woods except her soft moan of surrender.

Hunter devoured her. He commanded. He conquered. The soft carpet of grass received them as he lowered her to the ground. His hands shaped her miraculous body, memorizing the curves, teasing her nipples, exploring her sweet, secret places. She was his Mattie, his summer girl, his jazz, and he was intoxicated.

Mattie gloried in his touch. With her skirt bunched around her waist and her blouse gaping open, she writhed upon the grass. The splendor of Hunter filled her vision. He was dark and vivid and real. He was her passion, her dream, her love. And he was lost to her.

Like a knife to the heart, Victoria intruded. Her gaiety, her beauty, her pretty words, her final treachery, washed over Mattie, and she went slack in Hunter's arms.

He sensed the change immediately. His arms tensed and his jaw clenched. Damn you, Victoria, he raged silently. The passion ebbed from him as he tenderly cradled Mattie against his chest.

"It's all right, my love," he crooned. "I'm here."

For a while she clung to him, burying her face against his chest. It felt so safe, so good, she almost let go. But Mattie was stubborn, strong-willed, and determined. She pulled herself back and straightened her blouse.

"I won't take your charity, Hunter."

"Dammit, Mattie. That's not charity. That's love."

The black stallion, who had been peacefully cropping grass nearby, flared his nostrils and pawed the ground.

Mattie turned to look at the stallion. "Now see what you've done to the horse."

"Forget the horse. Look at me, Mattie."

She swung her head back around. Her eyes were as shiny as emeralds under the sun, bright with anger and love and fear.

"Don't you see, Hunter? Right now I'm empty. I feel unloved, rejected, betrayed. I can't deal with you and my mother at the same time."

He gazed off across the valley. He knew she felt those things. He knew she wanted to be alone, to work out her problem by herself. But he was afraid. Time and distance had played havoc with their lives once before. He wasn't willing to risk another ten years of loneliness.

With that resolution made, he turned to face her. "I won't let you go, Mattie."

He meant it, she thought. She could tell by the way the amber light burned in his black eyes. She could tell by the set of his square jaw, the thrust of his shoulders.

Excitement rose in her, hot and bright. It leaped in

her heart, spilled through her veins. Victoria was gone. There was nothing now except Hunter. But just when she would have reached for him, the flame of excitement burned low, and on its heels came despair. Her hatred of her mother was still there. Dreams couldn't be built on hate. It would haunt, distort, destroy.

Helpless rage filled her heart, and tears filled her eyes.

"Your not letting me go isn't love, Hunter. It's captivity." She jumped up, her fists clenched. "I will have no part of it." She turned her back on him and strode to the horse.

Hunter's jaw tightened. She had disappeared into her impenetrable shell again. The cold winds of despair blew against his heart, and he lashed out, as much against the hopelessness as against Mattie.

"Love!" he said. "How can you turn your back on me and talk about love? You don't know a damned thing about it, Mattie. You're too busy playing ostrich."

She whirled on him. "I am not burying my head in the sand. I see clearly, and what I see makes me sick! I'm being used, Hunter. *Used.* All my mother wanted was a little girl who would never grow up and make her feel old." She stalked around the stallion as she talked, waving her fists at the sky. "And all you want is somebody to satisfy your libido and warm your lonesome bed." She flung herself into the saddle. "If you're going back to the Rameau estate you'd better climb on."

"And put up with that stiff-necked, stubborn pride all the way back? No, thank you, Mattie. I'll walk."

She dug her heels into the stallion's flanks, and together they plunged through the forest.

Hunter watched them go. In spite of his anger, he noticed that her seat was firm and her grip on the reins sure. Mattie had always been a good horsewoman, he thought. There was no danger that she'd hurt herself. Damned stubborn woman. He unclenched his hands and rammed them into his pockets. God, how he loved her!

With that thought, he started his long walk back to the estate.

Mattie was still breathless with anger when she arrived at the stables. She flung the reins to the startled groom and ran toward the house. Getting away was uppermost in her mind.

"Jean-Louis," she called as she entered the house.

He came from the library, drink in hand, a smile on his face. He stopped smiling when he saw her. "What happened? You look like the wrath of Zeus."

"I'm leaving, Jean-Louis. I can't stay for the rest of the party."

"But Mattie—"

"There's no use arguing." Her foot was already on the staircase.

"It's him, isn't it?" Jean-Louis asked. "That pirate on the black stallion? Who is he, Mattie?"

"Somebody I used to love." She clutched the newel-post. She felt faint. She had to leave before Hunter got back, she thought. She couldn't risk seeing him again.

Jean-Louis took her arm. "Let me help you to your room. I'll have Clara bring you a glass of wine. Then we'll talk about everything."

"Just send Clara to help me pack, Jean-Louis, and order a car. I want to leave as quickly as possible."

Mattie didn't know how she got back to her apartment. She remembered nothing of the ride except the great ache in her chest. Her brain felt too big for her head and her arms were heavy. She looked at the unopened bags in the middle of her living room. She didn't even know how long she'd been back, how long she'd been standing there.

She moved slowly through her apartment, touching her furniture, straightening pictures on the wall, seeking assurance from her possessions that she was real.

Her piano gleamed through the evening shadows. She wondered when the night had fallen.

She sought solace in her music. She sat down at the piano and ran her hands lightly over the keyboard. They moved automatically into a melody. Its haunting beauty soothed her soul, restored her spirit. And when it was over, tears streamed down her face.

"Oh, Hunter! How can I let you go?"

Her bright hair fell across the ivories as she lowered her head to her hands. The hopelessness that had imprisoned her poured out in a heartbreaking wail. She cried for lost youth and lost innocence. She cried for lost dreams and lost happiness. She cried for Hunter, for herself, for Victoria. And when the tears had ceased she felt cleansed.

She rose from the piano bench, chin high and purpose lighting her eyes. Her steps carried her into her spare bedroom, the one Victoria and William had always used when they came to visit. She pushed open the door. The room smelled musty, like memories too long untouched.

She flipped on the light switch. The dust covers she had draped over the furniture after her parents had been killed in a car accident looked morbid and out of place. She jerked them off and tossed them into the closet. Then she sat down on the stool in front of the dressing table and picked up the few personal items there that had belonged to her mother—Victoria's gold dresser set, her cut-crystal perfume bottles, her ivory-inlaid powder box. All were the trappings of a vain woman, a woman obsessed with youth and beauty, and all of them felt cold and empty in Mattie's hands.

She opened the dressing-table drawer and pulled out a box of things that had belonged to her father. His favorite book of poetry, *Sunset Gun*, was on top. She smiled. That her generous and gentle father had loved the sharp, cynical verse of Dorothy Parker had always amused her. Could it be that he had admired the woman's way of cutting through to the truth of a matter?

As Mattie held the volume in her hands she realized that she'd never really known her father. He was such a sweet, easygoing man, always polite, always sitting quietly by, basking in the overshadowing beauty and vitality of his wife.

Had he known Victoria was selfish and vicious? Mattie wondered. Had he known she'd loved nobody but herself? How had he coped with it? How had he lived with that terrible knowledge? She delved through William's personal belongings—the pocket knife, the watch on a gold chain, the leather bookmark—until she found what she sought. Her father's diary. She'd never read it, had never wanted to read it until now.

It was locked. She searched the box for a key. Finding none, she took her father's pocket knife and pried open the rusty lock. The brittle pages crackled in protest as she turned to the first entry.

Her hair fell across her cheeks as she bent over the diary. She read the first entries quickly. They were bright, cheerful accounts of his courtship of Victoria and the early years of his marriage. She smiled when she read his account of her birth. The way he told it, he was the first man in the world to have fathered a beautiful daughter.

The entries then became skimpy. Months were skipped. A whole year was missing. The tone of the entries changed too. Gone was the cheerfulness, the joy. An occasional burst of happiness would shine through when he wrote about Mattie, but his references to Victoria were brief and strained, more like an appointment calendar than a diary.

Mattie set the book on the dressing table and rubbed her neck. Sitting on the stool had made her tense. At least, that was what she told herself.

She left the diary and went into the kitchen to make a cup of tea. She lingered over the tea-making as long as she could, measuring just the right amount of sugar, slicing the lemon just so. Then she carried her china teacup back into the spare bedroom.

She walked the floor, sipping her tea and watching the diary as if it might jump off the table and bite her. When she began to feel ridiculous and cowardly, she picked it up and carried it into her sitting room.

She took an inordinate amount of time arranging her teacup on the table beside her, plumping sofa pillows, and wiggling around until she had achieved the exact amount of comfort she desired. Then she opened the diary again.

Quickly she skimmed the next few short entries. Nothing important there. Suddenly she stiffened. William's thin, spidery writing began to fill the pages again. The entries were lengthy and detailed, and the tone was bleak.

Mattie's hands trembled as she read the words her father had written about her mother. "I know," the first long entry said.

I know about Victoria's men. All these years I told myself they were harmless flirtations, silly amusements of a lively woman. But I saw them today, that new cameraman and Victoria. I went to the studio early. She'd be working late, doing magazine layouts, she'd said. Lies! It was all lies. They were together on the set, arms and legs entangled, lips devouring each other, their cries enough to destroy my soul. I felt an urge to kill. Instead I stepped back into the shadows and watched, hoping it was somebody else, hoping I'd been wrong. I wasn't. It was my wife, my beautiful, vivacious, glorious wife, heart of my heart and soul of my soul. Sick. I walked out the door.

Mattie closed her eyes. She thought she might be ill. She started to fling the diary away, then she made herself continue reading. It was time to face the truth. She wouldn't let Victoria turn her into a shadow, the way she had William.

"I guess I've known all these years," William's next entry read.

The way my father looks at me sometimes, with sadness and pity. How I hate the pity. He's polite to Victoria, but I see the contempt he tries to hide behind good manners. He doesn't understand. He doesn't know the *real* woman I love. Victoria is like a little child. She's vain and spoiled and petted, but underneath she's scared. Sometimes when she curls up in my lap, she tells me that she's afraid to grow old. In her world, the world of poverty that I took her away from, old people are shunted off to horrible places and left to die. Sometimes she tells me that her beauty is her salvation. It got her out of the slums and it's all that keeps her out of the gutter. I cringe when she says that. How close she is to the truth! She gets out of my lap and strips off her clothes. Her body is perfection. "Look at me," she says. "Tell me I'm not getting flabby and old. Tell me I could make a living with this body if I had to." She won't believe she has nothing to worry about. She won't see that we're rich. Sometimes she sees the hurt in my face. Then she falls on her knees and puts her head in my lap. "William, you're the only man I'll ever love. The only one." I believe her. "What would I do without you and Mattie?" she says. "My Mattie. I love you both more than life itself. Don't ever leave me, William." I won't. She *does* love us. As much as she is capable, she loves Mattie and me. I assure her I won't leave her. Why can't she believe me? Why can't she trust my love?

Mattie laid the open diary on the table and picked up her teacup. The tea was cold. She didn't care. She'd seen the words. Her father would never lie. Her mother had loved her. She set down the cup and picked the diary up again.

The next entry was short.

I wish I could fill the great void inside Victoria. I wish I knew how to stop the ache that makes her continue to reach out to other men. But she can't stop. It's a sickness that consumes her. All I can do is forgive, and try to understand, and to keep on loving her, loving my beautiful, flawed Victoria. Sometimes I think my sanity hinges on this truth: We forgive those we love.

That truth shouted out to Mattie. It rose from the silent pages and resounded in the quiet room. It was the answer. It was the key for closing the door on Mattie's past and unlocking the one on her future. "We forgive those we love." Her father's serenity had been real, she thought, for he'd learned the art of forgiveness.

She closed the book and placed it on the table. Just as she'd once forgiven Hunter for what she thought he'd done, she must now forgive her mother. That was much harder. It meant admitting Victoria's guilt, seeing her clay feet.

Mattie jumped up and paced the floor, stopping every now and then to take a sip of cold tea. Tension coiled in her and made the back of her neck ache. She longed to go to her piano. She longed to drown herself in the forgetfulness of music. But determination held her back. Her future was at stake. If she didn't face this truth now, she never would.

The thought frightened her. What if she refused to acknowledge Hunter's love, just as Victoria had refused to acknowledge William's? Would she then truly become like Victoria, loose and amoral?

Mattie lost track of time. The moon trailed across the sky, and the rest of Paris slept in the shrouded darkness of apartments and homes. But in Mattie's apartment the lights stayed on and the teapot stayed warm. She drank fresh tea and paced the floor, thinking, thinking of William's love for Victoria, thinking of forgiveness. And at last the heavy burden was lifted from her heart. Scrunched in the corner of her sofa with yet another cup of tea in her hands, she forgave her mother. She accepted Victoria's flaws, her betrayal, her limited capacity for love. On the heels of acceptance came the good memories—the time she'd cried because her strawberry ice cream had fallen from the cone onto the sidewalk and Victoria had hired the ice-cream vendor to bring his wagon to their house every day for the rest of the summer so she'd never be out of strawberry ice cream; the champagne party Victoria had given in celebration of her first concert; the real pride she'd taken in Mattie's talent.

The teacup rattled against the saucer as Mattie set it on the table. Her head slumped back onto the sofa cushions and she slept.

Mattie squinted against the bright light pouring into the room. Her head ached, her back felt stiff, and her tongue was dry. She decided twenty-eight was too old. She lay on the sofa, glaring at the morning light and wishing the day would go away. Then her gaze fell on the diary. Energy surged through her, and she decided the day was wonderful after all. She smiled at the sun, she smiled at the diary, and she even smiled about her headache.

Mattie moved with unusual haste for someone who hated mornings. She had to call Hunter. Halfway across the room, she stopped. What would she say to him? "I've forgiven my mother"? "I've finally made peace with the past"? That sounded so trite. How could words make up for all the hurt?

She didn't even know where he was. She'd left him stranded in the woods on Jean-Louis's estate. For all she knew, he'd gone back to Dallas. And she wouldn't have blamed him if he had. Heaven knows, she'd been abominable.

She pressed her hands to her throbbing temples. Indecision and the possibility of losing Hunter almost overwhelmed her. As always when she was troubled, she sought solace in her music. Her hands touched the keyboard, tentatively at first and then with increasing confidence. The music soothed her soul, restored her spirit.

Finally she knew what she must do. No mere phone calls for her. She and Hunter had always done things on a grand scale. It was only fitting that they should begin a lifetime together in the same grand style.

She rose from the piano and made a few discreet phone calls. She felt like bending down and kissing the ground when she discovered that Hunter was still in Paris. Smiling, she put the rest of her plan into action.

The invitation was delivered to Hunter on a silver tray.

When he had first heard the knock on his hotel door, he'd been tempted to roll over in bed and ignore it. But some sixth sense had told him to answer the door. Now he was glad he had. He wouldn't have missed this show for anything in the world. The messenger boy looked like someone straight out of King Arthur's court. Hunter decided he must be hot as hell in all that armor.

He opened the gilt-edged envelope. One eyebrow cocked upward as he read the invitation. He was to be the guest of honor at a Mattie Houston concert, was he? Was it to be her finale? Her way of saying good-bye? His jaw clenched at the thought. Not if he could prevent it, he decided.

The messenger boy interrupted his thoughts. "I'm to bring back a reply, sir."

"Tell the lady . . ." Hunter paused, smiling. Such an elaborate invitation deserved an elaborate reply. He crossed the room and rummaged around in his suitcase until he found what he wanted—a teddy bear. Hastily he scribbled a note and tied it to the ribbon around the bear's neck. "Don't tell the lady anything. Give her this."

Mattie had already read the note three times. Hugging the teddy bear, she read it again. "Be careful, Mattie. Bears eat people."

Her hand clenched the note. "Please let this mean what I think it does," she prayed aloud. "Please let Hunter still be my teddy-bear man."

She lifted her head in a regal gesture. Hunter was coming. That was all she needed to know. She'd won him twice; she could do it a third time if necessary.

Placing the teddy bear on her bedside table, she began her preparations for the very special concert.

Mattie shimmered when she walked onstage. Her fire-and-gold hair was swept up and caught with a diamond clasp. The champagne-colored bugle beads on her dress—the one Hunter loved—shot prisms of light around her.

She was proud, elegant, poised. She was Mattie Houston, queen of jazz. Turning toward the audience, she smiled.

Hunter's hopes soared. The smile was for him, and him alone. He swiveled his head to assure himself that he was correct. A sea of empty seats met his gaze. He was not only the guest of honor; he was the *only* guest. There was no doorman, no box-office manager. He glanced upward. There was nobody working the lights. He and Mattie were completely alone in the concert hall.

He leaned forward in his seat as she began her first song. The melody seemed to flow from her. She leaned over the piano, caressing the keys. Her body moved with the rhythm. She was beauty, she was magic, she was music.

And the song she played was "Summer Wind."

Every note vibrated in Hunter's heart. It was their song. This wasn't good-bye, he thought. It was hello. It was commitment. It was forgiveness. It was the future.

He had to restrain himself from running onstage and taking her in his arms. He had to be sure this time. He settled back in his seat. A lifetime couldn't be built on a song. He would wait.

When the song ended, Mattie rose from the piano bench and bowed.

Hunter clapped. The sound was hollow in the almost-empty auditorium.

Mattie stood onstage and waited. Her heart was hammering so against her rib cage, she could barely breathe. He would come forward now, she thought. The song was significant. He would *know*.

Hunter's fists clenched as he sat in his seat, waiting.

She shaded her eyes against the spotlight. "Hunter? Are you still out there?"

"I'm here, Mattie."

"The song was for you."

"Was it?"

She stilled the panic that rose in her. She would not lose Hunter now, she vowed fiercely.

"It's our song, Hunter. It's always been our song."

"We can't build a marriage on a song." Still quelling his urge to run onstage, he stood and faced her. "That is what you're talking about, isn't it? Marriage? A lifetime commitment?"

"Yes."

"Then say the words." They faced each other across the vast emptiness—the teddy-bear man and his summer-jazz woman. Hunter's face softened. "I loved the clever way you had the invitation delivered. I love being the only guest at a special concert. But no more games, Mattie. Just the truth."

"I've reconciled myself to the past, Hunter. I read Daddy's diary. It made so many things clear. I've forgiven my mother. I've forgiven myself for all the wasted, empty years." She took a step forward. "I love you, Hunter, and I'll never, *ever* forget that again." She took another step, and another. "I need you, Hunter."

He was already in the aisle, and then they were both running toward each other. Hunter was quicker. He caught Mattie on the steps of the proscenium.

"I've waited a lifetime to hear you say that," he said as he hugged her to his chest. His lips were in her hair, on her cheek, on her throat. "I'll never let you go again."

She clung to his broad shoulders, smiling. "Remember that summer ten years ago? This is the end of our dreams, Hunter."

He lifted his head and smiled at her. "The end?" His mouth covered hers, and after a very long time he looked at her again. "Mattie, the dream is just beginning."

He scooped her into his arms and carried her back up the steps. "The prelude was yours. The encore is going to be mine."

He set her on her feet and reached for her zipper.

She smiled as the dress landed in a shimmering heap at her feet. "Onstage, Hunter?"

He pulled her back into his arms. "I've always wanted to be the star of your show."

Her hips rubbed against his. "You call that a star? I'd call it—"

He lowered her to the stage floor. "Be quiet or you'll miss the music."

THE EDITOR'S CORNER

Seven is supposed to be a lucky number . . . so look for luck next month as you plunge into the four delightful LOVESWEPT romances and the second trilogy of the Delaney series. Has the Free Sampler of **THE DELANEYS OF KILLAROO** made you eager to read the full books? (Whenever we do a book sampler I get the most wonderful letters of protest! Many of them very funny.) As you know from the creative promotion we've done with Clairol® to help them launch their new product, PAZAZZ® SHEER COLORWASH will be available next month when the Delaney books, too, are out. Think how much fun it would be to do your own personal make-over in the style of one of the heroines of **THE DELANEYS OF KILLAROO**! *Adelaide, The Enchantress* by Kay Hooper has hair like *Sheer Fire; Matilda, The Adventuress* by Iris Johansen has tresses with the spicy allure of *Sheer Cinnamon; Sydney, The Temptress* by Fayrene Preston has a mystery about her echoed in the depths of her *Sheer Plum* hair color. Enjoy this big three!

And for your four LOVESWEPTS, you start with **A DREAM TO CLING TO,** LOVESWEPT #206. Sally Goldenbaum makes her debut here as a solo author—you'll remember Sally has teamed up in the past with Adrienne Staff—and has created a love story that is filled with tenderness and humor and great passion. Brittany Winters is a generous, spirited woman who believes life should be taken seriously. This belief immediately puts her at odds with the roguishly handsome Sam Lawrence, originator of "Creative Games." Sam is a wanderer, a chaser of dreams . . .

(continued)

and a man who is utterly irresistible. (What woman could resist a man who calls her at dawn and tells her to watch the sunrise while he whispers words of love to her?) **A DREAM TO CLING TO** is an enchanting book that we think you will remember for a long time.

PLAYING HARD TO GET, LOVESWEPT #207, is one of Barbara Boswell's most intriguing stories yet. Slade Ramsey is the proverbial nice guy, but, jilted by his fiancee, he got tired of finishing last. Figuring women really did prefer scoundrels, he tried hard to become one. However, he was only playing the part of a charming heartbreaker, and he never got over the love he felt for the first woman he had treated badly—young and innocent Shavonne Brady. When he comes face to face with Shavonne, gazing again into her big brown eyes and seeing the woman she has become, Slade knows he can never leave her again. But how can he convince her that the man she knew a few years ago—the one who had broken her heart—isn't the real Slade? Barbara has written a truly memorable story, and not only will you fall in love with Shavonne and Slade, but all of their brothers and sisters are unforgettable characters as well.

In **KATIE'S HERO** by Kathleen Creighton, LOVE-SWEPT #208, Katherine Taylor Winslow comes face to face with Hollywood's last swashbuckling star, Cole Grayson. Katie is a writer who always falls in love with the heroes of her novels. Now she's doing a biography of Cole . . . and he's the epitome of a hero. How can she fail to fall for him? Katie and her hero are as funny and warmhearted a pair as you're ever likely to find in a romance, and we think you are going to be as amused by Katie as a tenderfoot on Cole's ranch as

(continued)

you are beguiled by the tenderness of a hero who's all man. This book is a real treat!

Only Sara Orwig could turn a shipwreck into a romantic meeting, and she does just that in **VISIONS OF JASMINE,** LOVESWEPT #209. After the ship she and her fellow researchers were on sinks, Jasmine Kirby becomes separated from her friends, alone in her own lifeboat. She is thrilled when she is rescued, but a little dubious about the rescuer—a scruffy sailor with a hunk's body and a glint in his eye that warns her to watch out for her virtue. Matthew Rome is bewitched by Jasmine, and begins to teach her how to kick up her heels and live recklessly. When they meet again in Texas, Jasmine is astounded to discover that the man she'd thought was a charming ne'er do well actually lives a secret and dangerous life.

Four great LOVESWEPTs and three great Delaney Dynasty novels . . . a big Lucky Seven just for you next month.

With every good wish,

Sincerely,

Carolyn Nichols

Carolyn Nichols
  Editor
LOVESWEPT
Bantam Books, Inc.
666 Fifth Avenue
New York, NY 10103

It's a little like being Loveswept

SHEER MADNESS

SHEER COLOR

SHEER PASSION

SHEER EXCITEMENT

SHEER INTRIGUE

SHEER ROMANCE

All it takes is a little imagination and more Pazazz.®

Coming this July from Clairol…Pazazz Sheer Color Wash —8 inspiring sheer washes of color that last up to 4 shampoos.

Look for the Free Loveswept *THE DELANEYS OF KILLAROO* book sampler this July in participating stores carrying Pazazz Sheer Color Wash.

NEW!

Handsome Book Covers Specially Designed To Fit Loveswept Books

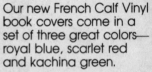

Our new French Calf Vinyl book covers come in a set of three great colors— royal blue, scarlet red and kachina green.

Each 7" × 9½" book cover has two deep vertical pockets, a handy sewn-in bookmark, and is soil and scratch resistant.

To order your set, use the form below.